"I Never Play With Fire."
She Paused.
"I've Never Met Fire Before."

Every muscle in Sawyer's body clenched tight.

He couldn't shake the feeling that he was being manipulated. But he also couldn't figure out why. She didn't know who he was, or she'd already have run for the hills.

"We have to go back," he told her. If they didn't leave now, he was going to kiss her all over again.

"Thanks," she told him softly, innocently, all traces of teasing replaced by sincerity. "For everything."

Sawyer turned for the shore, ruthlessly switching his mind to his uncle's dilemma and the dire price his family would pay if he failed. He couldn't afford to lose focus.

He couldn't afford to let Niki get under his skin.

Dear Reader,

Welcome to book four of the Colorado Cattle Baron series. With each story, I'm enjoying the Terrell and Jacobs families more and more.

In *Millionaire in a Stetson,* the Terrell brothers discover they have a secret half sister. Niki Gerrard is in serious trouble and runs to her newly discovered half brothers to hide out under a secret identity. Washington, D.C., mover and shaker Sawyer Layton, using a disguise of his own, tracks her down in Lyndon Valley to save his family from ruin.

In this day and age of technology and social media, knowing how many people are reuniting with their own family members, it was great fun to write a secret sibling story. I hope you enjoy it!

Barbara

BARBARA DUNLOP

MILLIONAIRE IN A STETSON

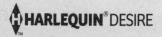

Recycling programs
for this product may
not exist in your area.

ISBN-13: 978-0-373-73237-1

MILLIONAIRE IN A STETSON

Books by Barbara Dunlop

Harlequin Desire

Silhouette Desire

*Montana Millionaires: The Ryders
†Colorado Cattle Barons

Other titles by this author available in ebook format.

BARBARA DUNLOP

writes romantic stories while curled up in a log cabin in Canada's far north, where bears outnumber people and it snows six months of the year. Fortunately she has a brawny husband and two teenage children to haul firewood and clear the driveway while she sips cocoa and muses about her upcoming chapters. Barbara loves to hear from readers. You can contact her through her website, www.barbaradunlop.com.

Prologue

In a magnificently appointed private room at the Seabreeze Hospital in Washington, D.C., Niki Gerard held her sleeping mother's pale hand.

The hospital specialized in discreet service for wealthy clients, so plush sofas replaced vinyl, institutional chairs, while the walls were painted in rich colors, adorned with original art and ornate crown moldings. An armoire held Gabriella Gerard's designer nightwear and robes. And a forty-inch plasma screen, which was connected to a keyboard for email and internet access hung on the far wall. Beneath it, there was a comfortable day bed, should a relative wish to spend the night.

But nothing could completely hide that this was a medical facility. A heart monitor beeped softly next to the bed, green numbers counting off, sending up corresponding spikes on the little graph in the background. An IV bag dripped morphine into the back of that hand of Gabriella's. She was too thin, only five pounds from her ideal weight, but Niki had discovered during these past two weeks that thin from a healthy diet and exercise looked different than thin from illness.

At forty years old, her mother had contracted a rare virus. She'd barely survived the high fever, and the ordeal had weakened her heart, also taking a toll on her aorta.

Gabriella's brilliant blue eyes fluttered open.

"Niki?" She appeared both confused and fearful.

"I'm here, Mom."

Gabriella convulsively squeezed Niki's hand. "Protect yourself."

"I'm fine." Niki gave her mother's hand a gentle stroke of reassurance. "You need to rest, not to worry about me."

Gabriella's gaze darted around the room, and she stage whispered, "You know where the money is?"

"You told me yesterday." Niki nodded. "It's in Switzerland."

"You'll need it."

Niki knew the size of her mother's investments here in D.C., so the statement didn't make sense. Not unless Niki had plans to buy a luxury hotel or a cruise ship in the near future.

"Tell me," Gabriella insisted.

"My birthday, your birthday and our building address." Niki repeated the code to access the account.

She'd hoped the increased morphine would calm her mother, not make her more agitated.

"Don't let them get it," Gabriella gasped.

"Who would get it?"

"Don't trust them. Don't trust any of them."

"Mom. It's fine. Everything's fine. Nobody can get the money."

"I mean it, Niki. The diary is your only hope. It'll keep you safe, keep them from…" Gabriella seemed confused again. "Wilton." She sighed. "How I wish…"

The diary? Gabriella was worried about her diary? Though she'd never seen it, Niki knew her mother had kept a diary for many years. She'd joked about the power of its secrets, mocking the married men who'd had affairs with her.

Gabriella focused intently on Niki now, leaning up. "They know. Too many people know—" Her blue eyes suddenly went wide. She cried in obvious pain, collapsing back on the bed.

Niki rose from her chair. "Mom?"

"Don't let them get the diary." Gabriella sucked in a few sharp breaths, then her jaw clenched tight.

Niki's throat closed over, and her chest ballooned with fear. She reached for the nurse's call button, pressing it hard with her thumb. "Mom?"

Gabriella's eyes blinked open, but there was something wrong. Her pupils were huge, and her brilliant blue irises had become translucent.

Two hot tears rolled down Niki's cheeks. "The nurse is coming. Hang on, Mom."

But the breath eased out of Gabriella's lungs. Then, just like in the movies, the heart monitor screeched out a solid beep. The line went flat.

Within seconds, two nurses sprinted into the room.

They crowded the bed, firmly elbowing Niki out of the way. She barely remembered to breathe as Gabriella's hand slipped from hers. Her brain fogged over in a daze.

An eternity seemed to pass, people coming and going, calling instructions to each other. But then, the urgency left their movements. Their voices went calm. Someone gently pulled the sheet over her mother's face. And a nurse led Niki to a chair in the hallway.

Gabriella was gone. Niki's beautiful, vivacious, irrepressible, fun-loving mother had died far too soon.

Niki felt a shiver run up her spine, and she had an eerie sensation of being watched. For a split second, Niki believed in ghosts. But then she glanced down the hallway to find a man in a business suit staring hard in her direction. Before she could react, he turned abruptly, banging his way through a set of double doors.

Gabriella's words flooded back to her. There were secrets

in a diary, money in a Swiss bank account and a mysterious *them* for Niki to worry about.

"Oh, Mom," she moaned under her breath. "What did you do?"

One

The trouble with living a lie, Niki discovered three months later, wasn't that you might get caught. It was that, eventually, you wanted it to be true. And that moment came when Sawyer Smith arrived at her half brother's newly framed ranch house.

Late-afternoon sun rays slanted through the empty window openings, turning the dust flecks to sparkles, and highlighting planes and angles of Sawyer's striking face. He was neater than most cowboys, clean shaven, hair trimmed short. But his stance was easy, shoulders square, hands wide and capable.

Niki was crouched on the rough plywood floor of the kitchen, power drill in her hand. She was putting holes in the two-by-fours in preparation for running the electrical cables. Her jeans were dirty, the heels of her palms scratched and red. She had sawdust in her hair, and her serviceable, green T-shirt was streaked with sweat.

"I took possession of the Raklin place yesterday." Sawyer spoke to her half-brother Reed, his deep voice carrying across the open rooms.

Niki watched covertly between the studs of the skeleton walls. Reed was an imposing figure, broad shouldered, heavily muscled, at a height of six-feet four. But Sawyer held his own. He was a little shorter, a little leaner, obviously athletic. And he was cover-model sexy, with the most startling, deep blue eyes she'd ever seen.

"Welcome to Lyndon Valley," Reed responded, reaching out to shake Sawyer's hand.

Sawyer's gaze met Niki's, and she quickly refocused on her work, embarrassed to be caught checking him out. She revved up the drill and lined up for the next spot that had been marked by the electrician. She eased the bit through the fibrous wood, her arm vibrating all the way to her shoulder.

Up to now, she would have sworn she was only attracted to the urbane, classy type. But, apparently she'd reassessed. At some point, after her life had taken a one-eighty, forcing her to flee Washington, D.C., for the wilds of Colorado cattle country, cowboys must have started to look good.

Not that it mattered. Nobody was going to be remotely interested in her while she looked like this.

When she'd lived in D.C., her hair had been long, wavy blond, always cleanly cut and highlighted to perfection. She'd never left the penthouse without her contacts, perfect makeup, fine jewelry and designer shoes. She preferred cultured entertainment and five-star restaurants. Her mother had taught her that if a man didn't own a Mercedes or a Jaguar, he might as well ride a bicycle.

But that had been Niki Gerard. Here in Lyndon Valley, she was Nellie Cooper, innocuous half sister of Reed and Caleb Terrell. Her hair was cut short and dyed brown. Her sensible glasses were perched on a sunburned, slightly freckled nose. She hadn't worn makeup in weeks, and her blue jeans had cost twenty-five dollars down at the Lyndon City Co-op.

Nobody from her old life would ever recognize her. But then that was the point.

"Hey, Nellie," Reed called from the entry hall, his deep voice booming above the high pitch of her drill.

She released the trigger, and the motor whined to a stop as she glanced up.

"Come meet our new neighbor."

Niki hauled herself to her feet, conscious of her sweaty, dusty appearance, telling herself that it didn't matter. She was working on a construction site, not waltzing into the ballroom of the St. Regis. Sawyer seemed to scrutinize her as she approached, and she couldn't help but wonder what stood out for him. The dirt? The sweat? The glasses? The plain-Jane hair?

"This is my sister," Reed introduced, motioning her farther forward.

Though they'd met for the first time three months ago, Reed never referred to her as his half sister. Neither did his fraternal twin Caleb. From the moment the DNA tests had come back positive, Niki had been welcomed into the Terrell family with open arms. Her newfound brothers had turned out to be solid, smart, dependable men. And with every day that went by, she regretted her lies to them more and more.

She wiped her hands across the front of her jeans as she stepped her way around a pair of sawhorses and over an air-compressor line. "Hello," she greeted Sawyer, swallowing the hormonal reaction that grew more intense as she neared.

He gave her a brief nod of acknowledgment. There was some kind of a question lurking deep in his blue eyes, but it quickly disappeared, and his expression smoothed out.

"Sawyer Smith," he intoned in a pleasantly mellow voice, holding out his hand.

"Nellie Cooper," she returned, her own voice slightly breathless as his hand closed over hers.

His was warm, strong and commanding, sending pulses of awareness skittering along her nervous system.

"I just bought the Raklin place across the highway," he told her.

"Welcome," she managed, wishing the odd sensation would stop, wondering if he could feel it, too.

"You lived here long?" he asked.

"Born and raised," Reed responded. "From our three times great-grandparents on down."

Sawyer released Niki's hand, and she glanced over to Reed in surprise. She knew the ranch had been in the Terrell family for generations, but she hadn't realized just how long they'd lived in the Lyndon Valley.

"That's impressive," Sawyer told him.

"What about you?" Reed asked. "Are you from Colorado?"

"Montana originally." Sawyer shifted his stance. "Spent a little time in the military after college. I guess I'm coming back to my roots."

"Good roots to come back to," said Reed as his cell phone chimed. "Excuse me." He drew the phone from his pocket and raised it to his ear, listening for a second, a smile growing on his face. "Hey, sweetheart."

Niki knew it had to be his wife, Katrina.

Though it didn't seem to happen often, because each of the brothers had other homes out of the state, both Reed and Caleb were on the Lyndon Valley ranch this week.

Reed and his wife, Katrina, spent much of their time in New York City, because Katrina was a professional ballerina. Caleb's wife, Mandy, had grown up on the neighboring Jacobs spread, but Caleb had spent years in Chicago building Active Equipment, his heavy-equipment manufacturing business. He and Mandy now spent about half their time in Chicago, half in Lyndon Valley.

"Starving," Reed said into the phone, and he grinned at Niki.

She tried to pretend she didn't notice Sawyer studying her. She'd attracted her fair share of male attention in D.C., particularly if she was wearing something by Delwanna, and always when she was wearing her black Magnamis heels. But she couldn't imagine she was anywhere even approaching attractive at the moment. She hoped she didn't have dirt smeared across her cheek or something equally gauche.

Sawyer's black jeans were spotless, his boots polished to a shine. He wore a white, Western-cut shirt with black piping and black buttons, and his curved-brim Stetson was worn enough to look natural, but new enough to complement the outfit.

Unable to stop herself, she reached up and casually brushed the back of her hand across each cheek. A breeze rustled through the windows, bringing the scent of wild clover. A diesel engine fell silent outside, and a horse whinnied in the distance, blending with the gurgle of the nearby creek.

Reed pocketed his phone. "Katrina's on her way with the barbecue fixin's. My wife," he explained to Sawyer. "Care to stick around for a burger?"

Sawyer gave an easy nod of acceptance. "Appreciate the offer." He unbuttoned one of his shirt cuffs. "In the meantime, can I lend a hand?" He rolled up a sleeve, revealing a ropy, muscular forearm.

The man was obviously used to hard work.

"There's plenty to do," Reed responded. "There's a crew unloading lumber around the back."

Sawyer finished rolling up his other sleeve and tipped his hat back on his head. "Then I'll get right on it." His gaze returned to Niki. "Pleasure, ma'am."

He exited and disappeared around the sheeted, exterior wall.

Reed moved closer to Niki. "You got pretty quiet there, Nellie. Something about that man get to you?"

"I'm shy," she responded, telling herself Reed couldn't read her mind. He had no way of knowing she found Sawyer unaccountably attractive.

But Reed barked out a laugh. "That's your story?"

She shot him a mock, arched glare, intending to show him she didn't mind being teased. "And I'm stickin' to it."

But even as she uttered the cavalier words, she struggled to shake off her embarrassment. She couldn't help but worry she'd looked pathetic panting after a man like Sawyer.

Though Reed's wife was a Colorado native, Katrina had spent most of her life in New York. She was unfailingly gorgeous and glamorous. Caleb's wife, Mandy, was so healthy and beautiful that she looked spectacular in anything she threw on, including worn jeans and plaid shirts.

But Nellie Cooper didn't have a lot going for her. When she'd been Niki Gerard she'd had plenty of money and time to make the most of her looks. But when you took away all the trimmings, there wasn't a whole lot left.

Being plain Jane wasn't much fun. But Nellie Cooper was just going to have to suck it up. Because she sure couldn't afford to have anyone make the connection between her and Niki Gerard.

Sawyer Layton couldn't believe he'd finally found Niki Gerard. To say she looked nothing like her photo was a colossal understatement. He doubted he could have picked her out of a police lineup.

Coming around back of the half-built house, he found a flat-bed truck loaded with lumber. He greeted a trio of men who were unloading, located a spare pair of leather gloves then joined them in their work, while his mind mulled over the latest turn of events.

Niki was calling herself Nellie now. He wasn't surprised that she'd changed her name. But he couldn't help wonder how she'd convinced the Terrells she was their sister.

It was a clever enough plan, hiding out at a ranch in the middle of the Colorado wilderness. Convincing a well-established family to take her to their bosom was pure genius. From the perspective of ingenuity and sheer audacity, Niki was clearly Gabriella Gerard's daughter.

His first load was three sheets of plywood. He balanced them against one shoulder as he followed a short path to the growing stack beside the house. He then turned for another load, settling into an easy rhythm.

Like Niki, Sawyer was operating under a false identity. But

he hadn't lied about buying the neighboring ranch. And he hadn't lied about being from Montana. He'd been born there. A technicality, because his parents, D.C. residents, happened to be vacationing on the family's Montana ranch when his mother went into early labor. Still, over the years, he'd spent quite a few vacations at the ranch, learning how to work outdoors and picking up the rudiments of cattle ranching.

Sawyer had grown up in D.C., along with a brother, a sister and countless cousins in the Layton clan. His brother had become a lawyer, specializing in taxation, and joined the family firm. His sister was engaged to Miles Carter, a young Congressman from Delaware. Meanwhile Sawyer had graduated college with a degree in international affairs and joined the navy as an officer. He'd liked the discipline and camaraderie of the navy. He'd also appreciated the black and white codes of ethics and conduct.

Sawyer lifted another three sheets of lumber. He was starting to perspire under the late-day August sun.

Unfortunately, his extended family had missed him while he was away. They'd missed his ingenuity, his nerve and his rather eclectic skill set. Since the Laytons had always been much better at getting themselves into trouble than getting themselves out, Sawyer had given up the black and white moral code of the navy for the countless shades of D.C. gray.

He'd gone back to work as the family fixer. Over the past few years, he'd done everything from misdirecting the press, to quietly paying off gambling debts and secretly locking extended family members in high-end rehab centers. But nothing compared to the latest trouble with Gabriella Gerard. When she had died, and then Niki disappeared, Sawyer's uncle, the senator had gone into full-blown panic mode.

Uncle Charles, along with many other power brokers in D.C., had a lot to lose if Gabriella's infamous diary saw the light of day. If that happened, the whole world would know Charles had cheated on his wife and, albeit unknowingly, accepted illegal campaign contributions.

Everyone knew that Niki had the diary. And now Sawyer had Niki.

"My brother tells me you're new to the neighborhood." A tall, dark haired man fell into step beside Sawyer.

Sawyer dropped his latest load down on the growing stack. "Sawyer Smith." He pulled off a glove to shake the man's hand.

"Caleb Terrell."

"Nice place you've got here," Sawyer complimented, gazing around at the lush meadows, rolling hills and the Lyndon River winding its way into the lake below. Befriending the Terrells was an integral part of his plan. He couldn't let Niki or anyone else be remotely suspicious of his reasons for being here. Luckily, Sawyer had enough money to temporarily buy a cattle ranch.

"We like it," Caleb responded, pride clear in his tone. "The main house is south along the river. But Reed's been planning this place for years."

As they spoke, Reed made an appearance in the front yard, joking with the men who were setting up a gas barbecue. He wrapped one arm around a petite blonde woman and gave her a kiss.

"His wife?" Sawyer asked Caleb.

"Katrina."

"Do they have enough kids to fill up this big house?" Sawyer asked in an effort to keep Caleb engaged in conversation.

"Not yet. Katrina's a professional ballerina, so it may be a while before they start a family."

From his research, Sawyer knew all about Katrina. Ironically, he'd seen her perform a few times in New York City. His family had a box at the Emperor's Theatre.

Niki appeared in the distance, joining the gathering group. She spotted a man setting up a folding table and quickly stepped up to help. Together, they drew down the legs and settled it firmly on the uneven ground. She was small and slight, only about five foot three. Sawyer also knew she was twenty-one, and she was partway through an arts degree at GW.

Niki had been drop-dead gorgeous in every picture he'd ever been shown, stunningly glamorous, one of D.C.'s own princesses. But there was no glamour about her today. Not that she could hide her pretty features. The wispy, brunette hairstyle made her look younger, delicate, a bit of a waif. The blue jeans clung softly to her sexy bottom, while the serviceable T-shirt molded to her breasts, making it anything but plain.

"I can see the way you're looking at my sister," Caleb remarked, in a light, yet warning tone.

"Sorry." Sawyer quickly shook himself. His mind didn't usually wander like that, particularly when he was investigating. He didn't know what was wrong with him.

But Caleb chuckled good-naturedly. "She's a beautiful girl. Just remember she's got two very protective big brothers in her life." He left the thought unfinished.

"Noted," Sawyer responded succinctly.

Caleb had absolutely nothing to worry about on that score. Niki might look sweet and innocent out here in the fresh air, but Sawyer knew what lurked beneath the facade. Niki was every bit as dangerous as her mother.

Both cunning and beautiful, Gabriella Gerard had used her persuasive charm and innate sensuality to get what she wanted from men who should have known better. She certainly wasn't a call girl, but her many lovers were strongly rumored to be amongst the D.C. elite. They had showered her with gifts, money, stock tips and, most significantly, secrets.

It was rumored that Gabriella had written it all down, and very likely included her affair with Sawyer's uncle and the illegal campaign contributions that had followed. Sawyer was here for the diary, nothing more and nothing less. Niki's virtue was perfectly safe with him.

"I guess I should have asked if you were married," Caleb put in.

Sawyer shook his head. "Not married. No girlfriend. Just me."

Caleb looked genuinely sympathetic. "Too bad."

Sawyer didn't think so. He was perfectly content on his own. Besides, family history proved that marriage was never a good bet for a Layton. He didn't think he'd inflict the state on any woman, let alone one that he cared about.

"Come and meet my wife," Caleb interrupted his thoughts.

They started for the front yard, with Caleb pointing out a woman in a pair of faded blue jeans and a red, plaid shirt. Her long, chestnut hair was pulled back in a ponytail, and she held a tiny infant in a blue blanket in her arms.

"Your baby?" Sawyer asked, falling into step, still making conversation about things he already knew.

"Better be," Caleb joked.

Sawyer couldn't help but smile at that.

"Mandy," Caleb called as they neared, fondness clear in his tone.

The woman glanced up. She smiled, green eyes shining with obvious love as the two men approached. "Hello, darling."

Caleb kissed her mouth, then he kissed the baby on the forehead.

"This is my wife, Mandy. Sweetheart, this is Sawyer Smith. He just bought the Raklin place."

Mandy's smile broadened. "Welcome to Lyndon Valley. This is Asher. Our new son."

"Congratulations," said Sawyer, looking down at the sleeping child. "How old is he?"

"Three months."

The baby's eyes were closed. His skin was almost translucent, and his little, bow mouth made gentle suckling motions in his sleep. He looked delicate and vulnerable swaddled in the flannel blanket.

It never ceased to amaze Sawyer that rational people would bring something so fragile into such an uncertain world. Didn't they worry about what could happen? How did they sleep at night, thinking about the danger?

Not that Lyndon Valley seemed dangerous. In fact, it was a million miles away from both political strife and inner city problems. And Caleb and Mandy were probably great parents, salt of the earth.

It occurred to Sawyer that a normal man would feel guilty lying to such obviously decent people. Luckily, Sawyer's emotions had been hardened over the years. But the thought led him to wondering if Niki was cold as ice, or if she was ashamed of her own deception.

He glanced up, seeking her out again.

She was looking directly at him, and when his gaze met hers, something arced through the atmosphere between them. It was an awareness that went beyond two strangers meeting. She quickly blinked and looked away, but not before it occurred to Sawyer that she might already have his number. Was it possible that she knew exactly who he was, and that she was playing him? Could she be that good an actress? He immediately realized he couldn't take the chance.

"He's a beautiful baby," he said to Caleb and Mandy. "Can you excuse me?"

He left them, making his way toward Niki.

She'd moved away from the crowd, going downhill toward the creek and a little white footbridge that crossed it.

He continued after her.

They had to have another conversation. And he needed to pay attention to more than just her beauty this time. If she even suspected he was a Layton, she'd bolt the second his back was turned.

Niki braced her palms on the rail of the footbridge, gazing toward the crystal-blue water of Flash Lake. Tiny ripples were signaling the beginnings of an evening breeze that would keep the flies at bay.

Flash Lake was surrounded by brilliant green willows and silvery aspens. Craggy mountains jutted up behind it, creating a picture-perfect setting against the vast sky. Closer in, horses grazed in the flower-dotted meadows, their black, brown and white coats, glossy in the rays from the setting sun.

Since it was midsummer, colts and fillies frolicked through the foot-tall meadow, their high-pitched whinnies carrying up the slope. Wheatgrass and clover freshened the air, while the crystal creek gurgled six feet below her, hiding water bugs and speckled trout. Though it had only been three months, there were moments when she had to struggle to remember the sights, smells and sounds of Georgetown.

But, not today. Today, D.C. was crowding out Colorado.

Niki knew the reason. Looking into Sawyer Smith's blue eyes, feeling what she'd felt, and wanting what she'd wanted, she'd been reminded that she was a fraud. She wasn't Nellie Cooper. She was Niki Gerard, daughter of Gabriella Gerard, the most notorious woman in the nation's capital.

That she shared a father with Caleb and Reed was nothing but a genetic coincidence. Her real life and her real world were far removed from their lives out here.

She hadn't given it much thought at the time, but now she knew she'd been wrong to bring her problems to their doorstep. She wished she didn't like them so much, or that Mandy and Katrina hadn't been so kind.

If she'd found her mother's diary, she might never have come here. If she had the diary, if she could read the entries, she'd know who to fear and how to fight back. But she'd searched every square inch of the penthouse, tracked down every safe-deposit box, checked every nook, cranny and corner. She'd even had a professional search through Gabriella's computer and email accounts, thinking the diary might have been electronic. But, no luck.

"Nice view," came a deep voice that sent an instant quiver up her spine. His footsteps sounded on the little bridge.

It took Niki a moment to find her own voice and respond. "It's beautiful," she agreed, praying Sawyer would keep right on walking.

But he didn't. He came to a halt and copied her stance, bracing his own hands on the painted white rail, gazing out at the lake.

"You're not hungry?" he asked pleasantly.

The aroma of grilling burgers was beginning to fill the air. Niki's empty stomach reacted to the enticing scent. She'd learned there was nothing like fresh air and physical work to heighten an appetite.

"Getting there," she admitted.

He was silent for a minute. "So, this is going to be Reed's house?"

Niki nodded, her attention going back to the two-story building.

"It's a big house for two people," Sawyer observed.

"Reed wants four children."

"Four?" Sawyer sounded surprised.

"I think he'd go for more if Katrina would agree." Niki had been present for some of their good-natured arguments. She couldn't help thinking about the way Reed looked at Katrina. He was head over heels in love, and Niki was sure he'd agree to anything she asked.

"What about you?" Sawyer asked.

The odd question surprised her. "I'm a long way from thinking about children."

Even if it did become safe for her to go back to her real life, she didn't think she was motherhood material. She certainly hadn't had any kind of a role model in her own mother. Gabriella was only eighteen when she'd given birth to Niki. They'd been more like friends than mother and daughter. And while Niki's childhood and teenage years had held more than their share of excitement, they'd also been chaotic and confusing.

"I was wondering if you might live here when the house is finished," Sawyer clarified. "You seem to be working hard on it."

Niki reframed her thoughts, coming back to the present, shaking her head. "That's not in the plan."

"You'll stay in the main house, then?"

Niki turned slightly to take in his expression, unsure of his

point. Then again, maybe she was simply paranoid and un-
comfortable thinking about her future.

Why on earth did Sawyer have to show up today? She'd
been perfectly happy living in this cocoon. It might not have
been ideal, but at least it was safe.

"Nellie?" he prompted.

She struggled to remember the original question. But then
she met his eyes, and her mind went completely blank. Another shot of desire raced through her system. He was a fantasy man come to life, all strength and purpose, silhouetted by
the mountains and the smooth blue sky. She suddenly wished
with all her heart that the life she had here was real.

Two

The ingenuous, puzzled expression on Niki's face told Sawyer two things. One, she hadn't the first clue who he was. And two, there was a reason his Uncle Charles had risked everything for an affair with Gabriella.

Niki's eyes were large, dark fringed, beautiful, clear green beneath perfectly arched brows. Her cheeks were pink, her face heart-shaped, and her mouth was a lush bow of red that telegraphed a lethal combination of eroticism and innocence. If Gabriella had even a fraction of Niki's enticing sensuality, Charles could be forgiven absolutely.

"Reed said you all grew up on the ranch." Sawyer changed the topic, intent on learning as much as he could about her cover story.

"Reed and Caleb grew up here," Niki responded, her attention going back to the view. "I'm their half sister."

"You grew up somewhere else?"

"Boston."

Boston, not D.C. It was only a slight alteration, and the

tactic earned his respect. Deception 101—keep your story as close to the truth as possible.

While they conversed, random shouts and the squeals of children crossed from the crowd of people around the house.

"A remarriage?" Sawyer pressed.

Niki shook her head. "Just me and my mom."

Another true statement. "Did you visit here in summers?"

"I never knew my father."

"Interesting story?"

"Not really," she said. "My mother passed away a few months ago. That's when it came to light."

"I'm sorry to hear that." On a human level, Sawyer couldn't help but be sorry that she'd lost her mother. His own mother had died when he was in his early twenties. Though the Laytons were never the most loving or attentive of parents, he still missed her.

"Thank you," said Niki.

They both fell silent.

"Do you wonder why she kept it secret?" he asked.

She shot him a curious look, and he realized it was time to back off.

"You must be hungry," he said, nodding toward the barbecue.

But instead of picking up on the topic change, her voice took on a faraway tone. "I came as quite a shock to them."

"Reed and Caleb?"

"Yes."

Sawyer quickly readjusted. "It must happen a lot these days. Strangers showing up, claiming to be relatives. You know, what with all the new social media and technology."

"And DNA doesn't lie."

"You took a DNA test?" Sawyer couldn't quite keep the astonishment from his voice.

"Of course. How else could we be certain? And, yes, I am hungry." She abruptly pulled back from the rail and started toward the crowd of people.

It took Sawyer a moment to recover. Niki was actually a Terrell? In addition to a dozen or so judges, politicians and captains of industry, Gabriella had slept with a rancher from Colorado.

It didn't fit her pattern. And, unfortunately, it meant Sawyer had just lost some of his leverage. He couldn't threaten to out Niki with Reed and Caleb if they were truly her brothers. That got him wondering if they knew who she was. Were they playing along with the ruse to protect her, or had she kept her true identity a secret from them?

If they knew the truth, then he was working against the entire Terrell clan, not just Niki. He scrambled to wrap his mind around that possibility. If they were all on alert, then a single misstep on his part would be a disaster.

He quickly caught up to her as she climbed the small rise toward the house. "You must have been excited to find them," he probed.

When she answered, there was a tightness to her tone.

"You mean because I went from being all alone in the world to having two of the greatest brothers in existence? Yes, I was excited to find them."

He tried to decipher her meaning. Were they great brothers because they were protecting her secret? "So, no other siblings?"

"None," she answered briskly, skipping into a jog.

She paused by a blue-and-white cooler, flipping the lid, dipping in to pull out a soft drink.

Sawyer hung back, pausing at the edge of the crowd.

"Travis Jacobs." Another cowboy stepped up and offered his hand.

"Sawyer Smith." Sawyer shook, forcing himself to regroup. More than ever, he knew he had to take his time with this. Finding the diary was going to be a marathon, not a sprint.

"I hear we're neighbors," said Travis.

"Word gets around fast."

"I'm Mandy and Katrina's brother. We have the spread that borders southeast of the Terrells."

"Mandy and Katrina are sisters?" Sawyer's research had told him as much, but the two women certainly didn't look anything alike.

"Jacobs, both of them."

And both married to Niki's brothers, which tied Travis to Niki, as well. If the Terrells and the Jacobs were anything like the Laytons, family was family, and they'd protect their own.

"Beer?" Travis asked, filling the temporary gap in conversation.

"Sure."

Travis crossed to the nearest cooler and extracted two cans of Budweiser, returning to pass one to Sawyer.

"The Raklin place?" Travis asked.

"That's the one."

"Good graze in the high country. Water issues in late September, but I expect you've looked into that."

Sawyer popped the top of his beer, letting his gaze focus on Niki as she spread mayonnaise on a hamburger bun then layered on slices of pickles. Katrina was beside her, laughing and chatting one moment, then talking low into her ear the next. He hadn't expected this much of a shield around Niki. In fact, he hadn't expected anyone to be close to her at all.

"I hear the water-license issue is going to be resolved soon," he said to Travis.

Travis laughed. "Anybody define 'soon' for you?"

Sawyer couldn't help but smile at Travis's skepticism. Truth was, the long-term viability of the Raklin place as a working ranch was the least of Sawyer's worries. He only expected to own it for a few months. Dylan Bennett, the ranch manager's son from the Layton family's Montana ranch had agreed to come out and run the spread in the short term to keep up appearances.

But as soon as Sawyer was done with Niki, his lawyers would put it back on the market. And, if the water license proved a stumbling block to selling, Sawyer could solve it with a single phone call. Charles might be the senator from Maryland, but he golfed with the senator from Colorado, and he had a whole lot of D.C. markers he could call in.

Assuming, of course, Gabriella's diary didn't get him kicked out of office and thrown in jail first.

"We've been fighting that particular war for a couple of years now," said Travis.

"Need any help?"

Travis arched a brow.

Sawyer took a swig of his beer, realizing it had been foolish of him to offer. "I know a couple of politicians," he explained.

"My brother was elected Mayor last year. I think he's got the political angle covered."

"Good enough, then."

There was no sense in taking on somebody else's fight. Sawyer's attention strayed back to Niki. He obviously had enough trouble on his hands.

"Since there is no earthly reason you would buy yourself a cattle ranch in Colorado," Dylan Bennett opened as soon as Sawyer came in through the front door of the Raklin place.

The man had parked himself in the living room of the ranch house, boots up on a worn, leather ottoman. "And since you're calling yourself Smith—unimaginative as hell, by the way. I'm guessing somebody's in trouble."

"We're the Laytons," Sawyer responded drily, pausing to plunk his Stetson on a wall peg in the entryway and rake a hand through his short hair. "Trouble is our middle name."

Dylan glanced around the expansive, recently updated living and dining areas of the big house. It was roomy and nicely finished, with gleaming hardwood, freshly painted walls, and a myriad of high ceilings, hewn wooden beams and panoramic windows.

"Pretty deep trouble," he drawled. "Judging by how much this place must have set you back."

"You always were smarter than the average cowboy," Sawyer drawled, moving into the living room.

"You want to catch me up?" Dylan stretched back in the worn armchair.

By contrast to the house, the furnishings were grim. They consisted of the leftovers the Raklins hadn't bothered to pack up, a worn brown sofa, a creaky armchair and a dated, arborite table with four mustard-yellow, vinyl chairs with spindly metal legs.

"You bring any beer?" Sawyer asked Dylan before sitting down.

"Stocked the fridge." Dylan cocked his head toward the kitchen where the Raklins had left four high-end, fairly new appliances. "Didn't make much sense to waste a trip through town."

"Good thinking," Sawyer approved, carrying on through the dining room to the kitchen.

He liberated a couple of bottles of Coors from the refrigerator door then made his way back to Dylan.

"It's Charles, isn't it?" asked Dylan as he accepted one of the icy-cold beers.

"What makes you say that?" Not that Sawyer had any intention of denying the truth to Dylan. Dylan was on their side. He'd been loyal his entire life.

As teenagers, the two men had run pretty wild together whenever Sawyer visited the Montana ranch. They stole liquor from the cook's pantry, borrowed more than one ranch pickup truck, got into fistfights and picked up girls. Their exploits had cemented a friendship, and Sawyer would trust Dylan with his life.

Dylan looked pointedly around the ranch house. "You bought yourself ten-thousand acres of prime land. As cover stories go, it's the very definition of overkill. I figure the only reason you'd go to this much trouble is to protect Charles' Senate seat."

"You nailed it," Sawyer agreed, dropping onto the old,

lumpy sofa and taking a swig of his beer. It was cool against his throat, dry from breathing in the dust of the construction site.

"You're blending," Dylan stated.

"In with the locals," Sawyer confirmed. He and his uncle had concocted the plan together.

"What the hell did Charles do to warrant this level of complexity?"

Sawyer knew he shouldn't smile. It was a serious situation. But Dylan was right, they were cleaning up a big mess with high stakes, and that situation inevitably involved Uncle Charles.

"You ever heard of Gabriella Gerard?" Sawyer asked.

"Can't say that I have."

"She was a D.C. legend, infamous around the town. Nobody knew where she came from, but everyone agreed she could have launched a thousand ships with one crook of her baby finger.

Word on the street is that she had affairs with some very powerful men. She accepted their gifts and their money, used their stock tips to get rich. She apparently squirreled away their secrets in a tell-all diary. And then she died. And the diary is nowhere to be found, neither is her daughter Niki."

"I take it Charles is featured in the diary?" Dylan guessed.

"And the daughter is featured in Colorado, in Lyndon Valley to be precise, in hiding."

"Is she Charles' daughter?"

"No chance of that. The dates were way off." Plus, Sawyer now knew she was Wilton Terrell's daughter.

Dylan gave a single nod of understanding, peeling at the corner of the beer label with his thumb. "You're here to get the diary."

Sawyer responded with a mock toast. "Indeed, I am. Charles would prefer his wife not find out he cheated."

"Understandable."

"He'd also prefer the Elections Commission not know about certain campaign contributions."

"Also understandable." Dylan took a swig of his beer.

"And he'd prefer to be the guy who learns everyone else's secrets, instead of the other way around. Whoever gets their hands on that diary will own the district."

"That all sounds like the Charles we know and love."

Sawyer silently agreed. He'd never had much time for the games played in D.C. politics, but Charles lived and breathed it. And he'd certainly done well by the family by being tapped in.

"This Niki might have plans of her own," Dylan noted.

"I expect she does. If she's anything like Gabriella, there's every chance she's planning some sophisticated blackmail scheme."

"So, here you sit," said Dylan. "Her brand-new, innocuous, cowboy neighbor, without a single, visible tie to D.C."

"That's the plan. Though we've hit a snag."

"Already?" Dylan glanced pointedly at his watch. "Is that a record?"

Sawyer ignored the man's sarcasm. "Those Terrell brothers I mentioned? Caleb and Reed. Successful men, smart from what I can see, a reasonable level of power on their own, particularly Caleb. It turns out, they really are her brothers, her half brothers, Gabriella was sleeping with more than just D.C. power brokers."

"Do the brothers know she's in hiding?"

"Haven't yet figured that out," Sawyer admitted. Though he was leaning toward them not knowing. "They didn't seem particularly suspicious or jumpy. They were happy to welcome me, feed me a burger."

Dylan rested one booted ankle on the opposite one. "So, what's your next move?"

Sawyer took another mouthful of the crisp beer, letting it slide its way down his throat. "Get to know them. See if I can find a way in. Getting her to confide in me would be best."

"Is she plain? Is she mousy?" Dylan gave him a critical once-over. "You're a decent-looking guy, maybe you can romance the information out of her."

"She's a bombshell. At least, she was in D.C. She's downplaying it out here. But I'm sure she still has plenty of offers." It occurred to Sawyer that one of the resident Colorado cowboys might already have his eye on her. That would add yet another barrier.

"Might be your best bet," said Dylan.

Sawyer frowned at his friend. Romancing a woman to get information from her? "That's pretty callous, even for a guy with my genetic make-up."

"Plus, if she's a knockout, what chance would you have?"

Sawyer gave a snort. "I can get dates."

"Sure, in D.C., where they know you're a Layton. I'm talkin' about out here, on your own, where women don't know you're a rich, connected guy."

"I'm not worried."

Not that he had any immediate interest in testing the theory with Niki or anyone else. His only goal was the diary. That would be his laser focus.

Niki knew she had to come clean with her brothers. She couldn't fool herself any longer, pretending it was okay to keep such an important secret. Though her mother would turn over in her grave at the thought of Niki taking such an unnecessary risk. In fact, Niki could actually hear Gabriella's voice inside her head, calling her a fool for giving up her advantage.

"Shut up," she said out loud, briskly rubbing her freshly washed hair with a towel.

She tossed the towel on a chair in the corner of the bedroom, then ran a comb through her short hair, scrutinizing herself in the mirror above the dresser as she worked. She had to admit, this was the easiest cut she'd ever worn. A quick comb through, and it dried on its own. It was just wavy enough to have body, but stayed pretty much in place through humidity or rain showers.

She stepped into a pair of comfortable jeans, then slipped her arms into a flannel shirt. She didn't even bother with a bra or socks. The lifestyle in Lyndon Valley was exceedingly casual.

The weather was sultry warm tonight, so she knew she'd find Caleb, Mandy, Reed and Katrina relaxing on the back deck.

If Caleb and Mandy were lucky, little Asher would be asleep, and there'd be time for an iced tea and some adult conversation. The river would rush by, and the crickets would chirp, and the scent of pine would flow down from the hillsides. On nights like this, Niki couldn't seem to imagine going home.

As the picture bloomed in her mind, her resolve to come clean began to waver. Maybe the confession could wait. After all, it had been three months already, what was another few days or weeks?

She had a deep-down fear of being rejected by her brothers, and she hadn't formulated a plan of what she'd do if Reed and Caleb kicked her out. Returning to D.C. and resuming her studies at GW was out of the question.

She was genuinely afraid of the men who saw her as a potential blackmailer. Not that she'd even think of blackmailing anyone. Even if she needed the money, she'd never commit a crime. And she would have happily told them all that—if she'd had any earthly idea of who they were. She remembered a few first names, but otherwise her mother had kept her romantic entanglements to herself and never shared the details with Niki. Perhaps her mom had been trying to protect her even then?

Yes, Niki was safest if she kept silent. But on the other hand, she shouldn't take the easy way out. Reed and Caleb had been so kind and so generous, they deserved to know exactly who they were helping.

She squared her shoulders in determination, leaving the bedroom and making her way to the staircase that led to the main floor. She tried to imagine how the conversation would go. Reed was a big, imposing man, but he was unfailingly fair and gentle. Certainly he'd been sympathetic to Niki so far, and she'd never once seen him raise his voice at Katrina or anyone else. Caleb was thoughtful, smart and doggedly determined. He worked hard and expected the same of the people around him.

Both of her brothers had high standards for themselves and everyone else. And she was fairly certain her behavior wouldn't have met those high standards. Would they merely be disappointed? Would they understand on any level? Would they be angry?

She shuddered at the thought of making either of them angry. Nor did she want to disappoint them, either. But their understanding might be too much to hope for under the circumstances.

Maybe if she'd been honest with them from the start. But back then they'd been strangers to her. And she hadn't dared share her secret with anyone in the world.

Now, as she cut the corner on the living room, she tried desperately to muster her courage. But as she pulled open the glass door to the deck, a heavy weight settled over her chest. Her heart struggled through deep beats, and her palms turned moist.

It was almost anticlimactic to find Katrina alone outside. She was lounging in one of the comfortable, padded chairs that overlooked a few lighted staff cabins near the river. The hills were black, and a million stars were scattered in the sky.

"Where is everybody?" Niki asked, half relieved, half distressed at having to wait even longer to bare her soul.

"In the barn. Lame horse. The vet's out there."

"Is everything okay?"

"It's not serious," said Katrina. "Just interesting." She paused. "For them."

Despite herself, Niki couldn't help but smile at Katrina's grimace. It was no secret that while the rest of the Terrell and Jacobs families were horse crazy, Katrina was afraid of the animals.

Katrina pointed to a bottle of merlot on the table in front of her. "Join me? I'm on Asher duty." She glanced up at an open, second-floor window.

"Sure." Alcohol sounded like a good idea. Maybe putting off the confession wasn't the worst thing in the world. There was every chance it would be easier after a glass of wine.

Katrina rose, selecting a second glass from the table and pouring the deep, red liquid.

Then she turned and paused on Niki's expression. "Everything okay?"

Niki's stomach tightened. "It's fine. Why?"

Katrina handed her the glass. "For a second there, you reminded me of Reed."

"You think I look like Reed?" Niki sure hoped not. While Reed was a ruggedly handsome man, he was all male, totally masculine.

"Every once in a while, I can see it around the eyes, and the way you purse your lips. He does that when he's worried." Katrina considered her for a long moment. "It reminds me that he inherited some things from his father."

"I really don't see a resemblance between us," Niki responded honestly.

She'd searched each of her brothers' features on more than one occasion, and she'd never been able to identify any similarities.

Katrina eased back down into her chair, gesturing for Niki to take the seat next to her. "It's more an expression than a specific feature. But don't tell Reed he looks anything like his father." She tossed back her hair and took a sip of her wine.

Niki followed suit, letting the warmth of the alcohol flow through her stomach and send an almost instant shot of relaxation into her veins.

"I doubt I'd get the chance," said Niki. "They never say much about Wilton."

She hadn't wanted to pry, and aside from pointing their father out in a couple of pictures, and having initially expressed their complete and utter disbelief that he might have cheated on their mother, both Reed and Caleb had kept their thoughts to themselves.

"They never will," Katrina said softly, her eyes clouding.

"I take it you know why?"

"I do. It's complicated. They had a very strained relationship."

Niki was sorry, if not completely surprised to hear it. There was obvious tension whenever Wilton was mentioned.

"Does it hurt them to have me here?" she couldn't help but ask.

"What?" Katrina seemed surprised by the question. "No. Of course not. This is your home."

Niki gave a sad smile at the irony. "It's not my home. I'm little more than a stranger to you all."

"No more a stranger than I am," said Katrina.

"You were born here," Niki returned. "Your sisters and brothers are here."

"So are yours."

"It's not the same thing."

The idea that Katrina could ever be considered a stranger to the Jacobs and Terrell families was preposterous. Even if she had spent many years at boarding school in New York City, Katrina had been the youngest Jacobs daughter her entire life. Everybody knew her. Everybody loved her.

"I spend most of my life away from here," said Katrina, continuing to sip her way through the glass of wine.

Niki was grateful, but she wasn't buying it. "I appreciate you trying to make me feel better."

"That's not what I'm doing. Well, maybe a little bit. It's obvious something's wrong. Are you feeling bad because you don't know much about Wilton?"

"I don't need to know much." Niki downplayed her curiosity. She desperately wished she knew more about her father, good or bad.

"The negativity and complexity have nothing to do with you."

"Whatever it is, I can handle it." The assertion was out of Niki's mouth before she realized it put Katrina in an awkward position.

"I'm sorry," she quickly added. "I didn't mean—"

"He was a cold, brutal man," Katrina told her. Her expression somber.

Brutal? "He beat them?"

"By today's standards, absolutely. But mostly, he was just plain nasty. He worked them into the ground, no empathy, no sympathy. Because of his temper, their mother died of pneumonia."

Niki had learned earlier that Sasha had died when Reed and Caleb were seventeen.

"The poor woman was so utterly afraid of Wilton, that she never told anyone how sick she was feeling."

Niki swallowed.

"Reed and Caleb both blamed Wilton for her death. To this day, they say he killed her. Back then, Caleb walked out, while Reed stayed to fight."

"I had no idea," Niki whispered, feeling a little numb.

Katrina topped up their glasses. "Of course you didn't."

Niki gazed at the dark liquid. She couldn't help thinking about her own mother, Gabriella's rather calculating, manipulative character. "Nice genetics I've got going here."

Katrina tossed her blond hair. "The genetics haven't done Reed any harm, nor Caleb, nor *you*."

Niki fought against the urge to confess who she was and what she was doing here. She might not beat anyone, but she certainly wasn't a very good person.

"My opinion," said Katrina. "Wilton was a phenomenon. All that bad blood running through his system, but he produced terrific kids. And you're part of the living proof."

"I wish I was," said Niki, her stomach cramping with guilt.

Katrina touched her hand. "You're looking like Reed again."

Niki struggled to smooth out her features, but the compassion in Katrina's eyes was more than she could bear. She had to tell her. She opened her mouth to speak.

"I'm going to make it better," Katrina vowed, carrying on before Niki had a chance to explain. "Here's what we're going to do. I was planning to go through the attic soon, to pick out some of Reed's things for the new house. You can help me. Who knows what we'll find out about your heritage up there."

Niki closed her mouth. It was tempting, so incredibly tempting to learn more about her biological family. But to do that, she'd have to postpone her confession. And that meant Gabriella won again—always a dangerous thing.

Niki gave her better principles one final effort. "I don't want to invade Reed and Caleb's privacy. If they'd rather I didn't—"

"That's not going to be a problem." Katrina waved a dismissive hand.

"They don't seem to want me to know," Niki added.

"They don't want to *talk* about it," said Katrina. "That doesn't mean they don't want you to know. Trust me on this."

"Trust you on what?" came Reed's voice as he opened the sliding door.

"Girl talk," Katrina responded easily. "Niki's going to help me in the attic."

"Yeah?" asked Reed. "You got an extra glass with that bottle of wine?"

"Absolutely," said Katrina with a broad, rather satisfied smile, gesturing to one of the tables. Then she gave a conspiratorial wink in Niki's direction.

Reed hadn't said no, Niki told herself. He'd barely reacted at all. Basically, he'd given her permission to snoop in his attic.

She took another sip of her wine, knowing she couldn't bring herself to turn down the opportunity. The truth would have to wait a couple more days. What could it hurt?

Three

Sawyer's Uncle Charles was chomping at the bit. A four-term senator, he'd had people snapping to attention for so many years, he'd long since lost any ability to summon patience.

In the ranch yard, Sawyer's tone was laced with disgust as he said as much to Dylan. "He doesn't see why I can't march across the highway, slam Niki up against a wall and demand she hand over the diary."

The mere thought of anyone putting a hand on Niki or any woman in anger, infuriated Sawyer.

"Subtlety was never his strong suit," Dylan responded, tightening the cinch on a bay gelding. The two men were outside the main barn, where Dylan was gearing up for a ride to survey the upper pastures. "But I do agree with the part where you march across the highway. You're not going to learn anything hangin' around here with me."

"I was over there just yesterday. I'm trying to play it cool."

"There are a million excuses you can use to go back."

"Like what? Borrow a cup of sugar?"

Dylan grinned. "Sometimes, I don't get why people pay you to investigate for them."

He freed the reins from the saddle horn. "Tell the Terrells you have a horse with a hot hock. Borrow some antibiotics until you can get into the vet's office. Or ask for the name of their vet. Or, hey, if you want to actually *be* useful, then find out where they hire their hands. Maybe they know of somebody who could be an assistant manager, help me out here." He mounted his horse.

Sawyer had to admit, those were all good suggestions.

"Or," Dylan finished, reining the gelding in a circle. "Pretend you like the woman. A lovesick calf would be expected to turn up all the time, on the flimsiest of excuses."

"I'm not going to do that," said Sawyer.

Niki might be a conniving little liar, but that didn't give Sawyer the right to behave like a jerk.

Dylan shrugged. "Good luck, then." He pressed his heels against the animal's flanks.

"Thanks." Sawyer stepped back, out of the path of the horse's dust.

Admitting he'd much rather spend his time trying to learn more about Niki than explaining himself to Uncle Charles or anyone else in D.C., Sawyer took part of Dylan's advice. He fired up a pickup truck and bumped his way down the ranch road, across the highway and up the winding stretch of the Terrells' driveway.

He debated whether to take the turnoff to the main house or carry on to Reed's new house, since it seemed likely Niki might be working there again.

Niki Gerard as a construction worker. Sawyer had to admit, he'd have bet money against that ever happening. She was obviously taking her charade very seriously, and he couldn't help but wonder if she was learning anything about life in the process. Well, besides how to work a power drill.

He checked with a hand in the ranch yard and was told the family was at the river.

Hoping Niki was included in the family group, he strode his way down a tree-lined trail behind the main house, hearing the sounds of talking and laughter before he saw anyone. He emerged from the woods to a picturesque meadow and a wide, relatively calm bay jutting out from the river. There was a gazebo in front of the sandy beach, which was strewn with lawn chairs and towels.

Caleb and Mandy, Reed and Katrina, and a number of people he didn't recognize were swimming and sunning themselves. Caleb was holding his baby son, but Sawyer's gaze immediately caught on Niki who was walking from the river's edge across the sandy beach.

Her dark hair was slicked back. Her skin glistened wet in the sunshine. Her blue bikini showed off toned, tanned legs, a flat stomach and smooth shoulders. The wet fabric clung to her pert breasts and to the curve of her hips. His feet slowed to a halt, and he simply couldn't drag his gaze away from the sexy picture.

She bent over a chair, scooping up a diaphanous scrap of nothing, wrapping it around her body. He knew it was supposed to cover her up, but the breeze pushed the sheer fabric against her body, and it just made her look sexier.

Her gaze caught his, and she seemed to startle.

He forced himself to resume walking. "Hello," he called to Caleb who was closest. "Sorry. I didn't mean to barge in."

"No problem," Caleb responded, shifting Asher in his arms. "Getting settled?"

Sawyer was aware of Niki moving in his peripheral vision, but he forced himself to keep his attention fixed on Caleb. "Slowly but surely," he responded. "My ranch manager arrived last night. This is a gorgeous spot you have here."

"One of our favorites. Mandy and I have to go back to Chicago in the morning, and she didn't want to waste the day."

"I don't blame her." Sawyer meant it.

"Join us for a dip," Caleb invited.

Sawyer glanced down at his blue jeans and boots. "I'm not

really…" Then he decided, to hell with it. He wasn't shy about his black boxers. And this was exactly the kind of excuse he needed to hang around. "Sure," he amended. "Why not?"

Caleb grinned. "That's the spirit. We're about to start a game of water polo. There's a stack of towels in the gazebo."

By the time Sawyer had stripped off his outer clothes and made his way to the bay, there were at least a dozen people positioning themselves in the water for the game. It turned out to be a modified version of regular water polo, with a volley ball and two floating nets. His navy background gave him an edge, but Caleb, who was on Sawyer's team, and Reed, on the opposite team, were both strong players. Reed, in particular, could effortlessly lob the ball from one end of the makeshift court to the other.

Niki was on the opposite team, and she turned out to be a surprisingly strong swimmer. So, when she and Sawyer both went after a long pass, he had to kick it up a notch to stay ahead. He beat her by a couple of feet, just before the ball would have been grabbed by the current out in the main channel of the river. He snagged it and quickly tossed it back to his teammate Mandy, who put it into play to the cheers and shouts of both teams.

He'd just launched himself to swim back, when Niki gasped. He twisted his head to look back.

"Oh, no," she cried as the current grabbed her.

She stroked hard against it, legs kicking beneath the surface. Her eyes went wide as the current won and began to tow her away.

Sawyer lunged for her, swimming fast and hard, until he could grab her by the arm.

"My leg's cramping," she gasped. The water was much colder now that they were out of the bay.

Sawyer wrapped an arm around her waist, flipping her into a rescue position. "Relax," he instructed. "I've got you. I'm going to take us into shore."

To her credit, she didn't panic.

He glanced at the crowd in the water polo game. Reed had seen her flounder, and was beginning to make his way over to help.

"It's good," Sawyer shouted to him. "I've got her." He gave Reed a thumbs up, just as the current dragged the two of them around a bend. The water-polo game disappeared from sight.

Going with the current, he managed to angle himself and Niki toward the bay. "You okay?" he asked her.

She was gritting her teeth. "My left calf is seized up."

"That's the cold water. Just give me a minute here."

He glanced around to gauge their situation. The white water told him where there were rocks beneath the surface, but he could see a safe route he could use to get them to shore.

"Sure," she hissed between her clenched teeth. "Take your time. I'm not going anywhere."

He couldn't help but smile. "Thank you for not making this any harder."

"Thank you for rescuing me."

"My pleasure."

She rolled her eyes. "I'm sure it was exactly what you had in mind for your day today."

They were getting close to shore now, in a place where the current was weaker. "I trained for this in the navy," he told her. "It's probably good to keep my skills sharp."

As he spoke, he became aware of how her body was cradled against his, the slick, smooth skin of her midriff, her rear end rubbing against his body, and her pert breasts bobbing above the water. It had sure never been like this in the navy.

His feet touched the rocky bottom, but he kept her in his arms, turning her sideways to more easily hold her.

"It's warmer here," she noted, voice still strained.

"Shallower, and less current flowing through. The sun warms the water. How's your leg?"

"Pretty sore."

He ran his fingertips along the back of her left calf, easily finding the bunched muscle. "Here?"

"Ouch. Yes."

He rubbed the area experimentally with the pad of his thumb, zeroing in on the knot. She moaned, arms tightening around his neck.

"Helping?" he asked.

"Yes," she hissed, pressing her face into his wet shoulder.

He massaged slightly harder, and she clung tighter.

"Stretch your toes up," he instructed. "Arch your foot."

She did as he asked, and he kept up the circular motion. He could feel her muscle begin to soften under his fingers, and she relaxed against his chest.

He knew he could stop anytime. He'd probably given her as much relief as he could for the moment. But he didn't want to let her go. He wanted to hold her against his body a little longer, or maybe a lot longer, maybe forever.

He stole a glance at her face.

She was gazing up at him, those huge green eyes soft in the dappled sunlight. Her lips were dark and full, rosy cheeks damp with water droplets. She had the thickest lashes he'd ever seen. He couldn't believe a woman could possibly be this beautiful. She was like a spell, holding him enthralled.

The warm wind whispered against them, wafting the scents of pine and clover. The aspen leaves rustled above. The sound of the others' voices blending away in the distance. Her skin grew warm against his own, and the noise of the water lapping around them seemed softer.

He wanted to kiss her. He didn't think he'd ever wanted anything so badly in his life. It was stupid and wrong and colossally risky. But he couldn't bring himself to care.

He bent his head.

She didn't shy away. In fact, she stretched to meet him. Their cool lips touched, flaring instantly to heat. His lips parted. Hers followed in turn. She was sweet as fresh honey, soft as dew.

His arms tightened around her, and he felt her body arch against him. He was instantly aroused, desperate to possess her. His tongue delved deep. Hers answered, and she moaned against his mouth, her hands tangling in his wet hair.

They were wearing practically nothing. It would be so quick, so easy, so intensely satisfying to strip off their suits and become one.

But faraway shouts penetrated his hearing, and he ruthlessly reminded himself where he was, who she was and what was at stake.

With a superhuman effort, he ended their kiss. Fixing his focus on the far shore, he dragged gulps of oxygen into his lungs.

"I'm sorry." He glanced down.

Her sexy vulnerability was almost his undoing.

"I didn't mean for that to happen," he told her sincerely.

She was silent for a long moment. "It's complicated," she finally whispered.

"It's simple," he returned, struggling to keep it light. "Fear and pain produce intense emotional reactions. Sometimes our bodies don't know what to do with those emotions."

"You think that's what just happened?"

"I know that's what just happened." Not that it had ever happened to him before. Not like this, anyway. Her kiss had all but blown his mind.

She quirked a little half smile. "So, you're not really a good kisser."

"No better than average." He found his gaze dropping to her mouth, and he recognized just how desperately he wanted to do it again.

"That was average?"

Steeling himself against temptation, it took him a second to answer. "Yeah. That was average."

Her eyes took on a mischievous sparkle. "Then you must have a pretty fabulous sex life, Sawyer Smith."

His gut clenched. "Do you always play with fire, Nellie Cooper?"

"I never play with fire." She paused. Her expression going thoughtful. "I've never met fire before."

Every muscle in Sawyer's body was instantly taut. She was beyond good. When it came to seduction, this woman could write the book. Or maybe she'd read the book. Her mother's book.

He couldn't shake the feeling that he was being manipulated. But he also couldn't figure out why. She didn't know who he was, or she'd already have run for the hills.

Then again, maybe she did this to all men. Maybe it was as natural for her as breathing.

"We have to go back," he told her. If they didn't leave now he was going to kiss her all over again.

"Thanks." She spoke softly, innocently, all traces of teasing replaced by sincerity. "For everything."

Sawyer turned for the shore, ruthlessly switching his mind to his uncle's dilemma and the dire price his family would pay if he failed. He couldn't afford to lose focus. He couldn't afford to let Niki get under his skin.

In the attic the next day, Niki was still trying to wrap her mind around the effect of Sawyer's kiss. For her, it had been a mind-blowing, earth-shifting experience. The kind of kiss she hadn't even known could exist. For him, apparently, she was just another pair of lips.

She'd struggled not to feel insulted by his cavalier attitude. Surely her ego couldn't be that fragile. It wasn't as if she was hopeless in the romance department. Okay, it was true that she hadn't had a date since she'd left D.C. And her most recent college boyfriend had broken up with her a few months before that.

So, maybe it had been a dry spell.

In fact, she told herself, perhaps that's why Sawyer's kiss had made such an impact. It wasn't the kiss itself, it was her pent up lust from so many months of being alone. Yes, that made a lot more sense.

"This is their wedding picture." Katrina rose to carry a framed photograph to where Niki perched on the corner of the wooden crate, browsing through pieces of old, floral patterned china.

The attic was slightly dusty, but well-organized, each cardboard box labeled and stacked in a neat row. It was sultry warm, the air close from the midday heat. Streams of sunshine came through the paned windows, making geometric patterns on the worn, wood floor.

Niki accepted the picture, gazing down at a burly, stern-looking man dressed in a dark suit. Next to him was a small, slight woman, smiling in a full-length white dress. It was a simple, classic a-line with a scooped neck. Her bouquet looked as if it had been picked from the garden, and her veil was a single layer of gauze. But nothing could detract from the woman's beauty.

"So this is Sasha?"

"Yes, it is."

"She was gorgeous."

"I don't remember her very well. But I do remember thinking she was beautiful."

"It's hard to imagine she had a baby like Reed." Niki caught herself. "I mean—"

But Katrina laughed. "You don't think I've noticed my husband's size?"

"I didn't mean it to sound insulting."

"It didn't. Sasha was never even remotely robust. It's funny, not ha-ha, but ironic. When we first met again as adults, Reed nearly killed himself trying to stay away from me, because he was afraid this way of life would kill me, too."

Niki looked up at Katrina. "I thought he blamed his father."

"He does." Katrina's tone was quiet. "This place just gave Wilton the means to do it."

"Is that why Reed's so protective of you?"

Katrina seemed surprised. "You think he's protective?"

"Yes," Niki drawled, adding a chuckle for good measure.

"And hopelessly in love. I'd give a lot to have a guy watch over me the way Reed watches over you."

Katrina's cheeks were slightly red. "What about Sawyer?"

Niki stilled.

"It took him a while to pull you out of the river yesterday. And, when you came back to the water polo game, the two of you looked a little..." Katrina grinned as she waggled her brow.

"A little what?" Niki stalled.

"You know." Katrina nudged her in the arm. "A little shell-shocked and in awe of each other. Come on. Tell me what happened in the bushes."

"Nothing happened in the bushes," Niki answered honestly, feigning an intense interest in the wedding photo.

"Ha," Katrina crowed. "Then it happened in the river. What happened in the river?"

"Fine," Niki huffed. Over the past few months, she'd learned it was safest to stick as close to the truth as possible. The fewer lies she told, the easier it was to keep her story straight. "He kissed me."

Katrina's grin widened with glee. "Like how?"

"Like, with his lips."

"On your lips."

"You are *so* nosey."

"I'm the closest thing you have to a sister. Of *course* I'm nosey."

"On the lips," Niki admitted.

"Was it good?"

"It was great." Niki couldn't hold back an involuntary sigh.

"But?" Katrina prompted.

"I don't think it was that great for him."

Katrina settled next to Niki on the wooden crate. "Why on earth would you think that?"

"Because he said so."

Katrina drew back. "He kissed you, and then he told you he didn't like it?"

"He said it was, and I'm quoting here, 'average.'"

"Wait a minute." Katrina gave her head a little shake. "Walk me through that conversation."

"In detail?" Niki was taken aback by the request.

"Yes, in detail. How else am I going to give you my best sisterly advice?"

"This can't really be the way sisters talk."

"Yes, it is. And I have two of them. So, I'm the expert."

Niki was forced to concede that point. "Fine. He said pain and fear produce intense emotions, and that's why I thought it was a great kiss. Then he said he thought it was an average kiss."

Katrina's shoulders drooped, and she looked slightly deflated. "Oh."

"Yeah," Niki agreed. "I guess I'm not like you."

"Not like me how?"

"Sexy. Stunningly gorgeous, charming and kind. The type of woman who produces intense, undying love in the man of your dreams."

"You are, too," Katrina put in staunchly.

But Niki shook her head.

"I don't know what's wrong with that Sawyer Smith. You *are* stunningly gorgeous."

"And you're also very sweet. Which only helps prove my point about you."

Katrina scrutinized Niki's face. "I can't believe you don't know you're beautiful. People must have been telling you that all your life. Do you think they were lying?"

"I think they were seeing the clothes, the jewelry, the makeup and hair styling."

Katrina scoffed, "That's ridiculous."

"My mom did okay for money," said Niki, again sticking as close to the truth as she dared. "And she knew how to do glam. She went to a lot of expense to make me look pretty."

"And now that you're here? In your dusty blue jeans and your wrinkled T-shirt. What's your excuse now?"

"I rest my case. Sawyer characterized my kiss as average. I'm nothing special without the makeover."

"Let's ask Reed."

Niki burst out laughing. "He's my brother. He's your husband. What's he supposed to say?"

"He'll tell the truth."

"Honestly, Katrina. You grew up in New York City, how can you not know that men will lie to humor the woman they love? Or that they want to sleep with? Or to avoid an argument? Or really for any old reason at all?"

"Reed better not be humoring me," Katrina growled.

"He's not. But with me, I guarantee he would be. He wouldn't hurt my feelings for anything."

"Okay, Caleb, then."

"He's still my brother. Honestly, Katrina, this really isn't a big—"

"Travis."

Niki stopped.

"Travis is single," said Katrina. "And trust me, he's been brutally honest with me my entire life." She paused, her mind obviously speeding toward a conclusion.

"That's it." Katrina snapped her fingers. "Travis is single."

Niki's stomach lurched. "Oh, no."

"Oh, yes. It's a brilliant idea. You and Travis."

"You and your sister are married to my two brothers, and now you want to set me up with *your* brother? Bad plan, Katrina, very bad plan." Not to mention mortifyingly embarrassing.

"You don't need to worry about a thing," said Katrina.

"He's barely looked twice at me," Niki pointed out.

"He hasn't had a chance. We're all going to town tomorrow, Nellie. This is rodeo weekend."

"You like rodeo?"

"I hate rodeo. But I do like the Saturday-night dance. You and me?" Katrina pointed back and forth. "We're going to town early, and we're going shopping, and then we're going dancing."

"No." Niki flat-out refused.

"We are going to make you so drop-dead gorgeous, he'll never know what hit him."

Four

Niki might be at the Springroad Mall under protest, but it seemed that certain life skills had been burned directly into her brain. She simply couldn't help herself. She had quickly zeroed in on a sparkling gold cocktail dress in Blooms. She knew before she had it off the hanger that it would look terrific.

It needed a belt, black, to go with the black high-heeled shoes she'd spotted from thirty yards away. The low detailed neckline cried out for something chunky and shiny, and she knew she had just the right accessory with an onyx and crystal necklace, specked with gold dust. That it came with matching earrings and a bracelet was nothing but a bonus.

"You rock at this," Katrina grinned, folding a red satin dress over her own arm. "I don't need them, but I'm getting shoes, too."

"Of course you need them," Niki put in. "All women need shoes always."

"These?" Katrina held up a pair of impossibly high rhine-stone sandals.

"Yes! You've got such good balance," said Niki. "Must be all that dance training."

"I'm also short," Katrina complained. "And Reed is very tall."

"Reed *is* very tall," Niki agreed. "And Caleb's not far behind." She wished she'd ended up with a little of her brothers' height.

"Try it on," Katrina prompted, pointing to the gold dress.

Niki easily agreed. Thinking about her serviceable bra and beige panties, she snagged a white, lacy set on the way past a display.

"Right back," she told Katrina, her heart feeling light for the first time in months.

She snapped the heavy curtain closed and quickly kicked off her sneakers, stripping out of her jeans and T-shirt. She tossed aside her clothes and unzipped the glittery dress.

She couldn't help regretting her brown hair as she shimmied into the sexy dress, which clung to her curves and accentuated her slim waist. The hemline showed plenty of leg, and she stepped into the black sandals, liking the way they elongated her calves. The necklace was perfect, and she turned one way and then the other in the long, oak-framed mirror.

"Show me," Katrina called from outside the change room.

Niki ran her fingers through her hair, fluffing it up as best she could, before pulling back the curtain with a dramatic flourish.

"You're gorgeous," Katrina gasped. "Buy it. Buy *everything.*"

"You think?" asked Niki, catching a glimpse of herself in a distant mirror. She had to admit, she liked the look.

"But why didn't you say something?"

"About what?"

"Your sense of style. You're always wearing such plain clothes. You downplay everything." Katrina studied her new appearance from head to toe. "Do you have contacts?"

"Somewhere," Niki admitted, knowing she shouldn't, but

feeling incredibly tempted. If she was going to dress up, it was hard to go halfway. There had to be a spare pair of contacts squirreled away in her purse.

"Find them," said Katrina. "We're going for a makeover. Travis is going to eat his wor—" She shut her mouth, swallowing convulsively.

"Eat his what?" Niki couldn't help but ask.

"His hat," Katrina said brightly.

"You were going to say his words."

The guilt all but radiated off Katrina.

"What were his words, Katrina?"

"Nothing important. That necklace is spectacular on you."

"You have to tell me."

"No, I don't."

"If you don't tell me what he said, how am I going to know what I'm up against?"

"You're not up against anything." Katrina circled her, eyeing up the dress from every angle.

"Give," Niki insisted.

Katrina frowned and drew a melodramatic breath. "He said you seemed like the tomboy type."

Niki didn't know whether to laugh or cry. In creating Nellie, she was going for the polar opposite of her real self, and it seemed as if she'd succeeded. "I've never been called that before."

Then again, she'd never spent any time working on a construction crew, either. Her gaze was drawn back to the mirror. If not for the hair and glasses, she really would knock 'em dead in this outfit. The fabric was a viscose crepe, puckered to reflect the light, but tight enough to whet a man's imagination. The short hemline and the high shoes gave the illusion her legs were long, and the neckline showed just enough cleavage to be interesting.

She reached up to touch her short locks.

"Madeline over at Lush Cuts can do wonders," Katrina whispered.

"Do we have time for all that?" They'd barely started shopping, and it was after five already.

"Oh, honey," Katrina ushered her back into the change room. "The men will wait."

Three dresses, two pairs of shoes, and one hair trim later, Niki sat in a leather recliner, her feet soaking in a small tub of water.

"I told you Madeline would work wonders," said Katrina from the chair beside her.

"She must have magic mousse," Niki responded. She was amazed at how full and rich her hair looked. It seemed lighter in color, too, curling around her ears and along the base of her neck.

"You're beautiful, Nellie," said Katrina, squeezing her hand. "I don't know why you hide it so hard."

Niki's chest suddenly went tight. She closed her eyes, and for several minutes, imagined she was a little girl again. Her mother was sitting next to her, sharing a pedicure, touching her hand, telling her she was beautiful. It was one of Niki's earliest memories.

She felt her eyes tear up, and she blinked rapidly against the onslaught of emotion.

"Hey," Katrina sing-songed. "What's going on in there?"

"Thinking about my mother." Niki lifted her lashes, noting the look of kindness in Katrina's eyes. "She loved pedicures."

Katrina nodded her understanding. "What was her favorite color?"

"Fire-engine red. She liked it in a lipstick, too." A small tear escaped, trickling slowly down Niki's cheek. "She used to tell me red got a man's attention, and everything good in life started with a man's attention."

Katrina arched a brow. "Seriously? Was she that far behind the times?"

Niki couldn't help but smile. "That's a good way to put it. She loved glitz and glamour. I can easily see her with a long cigarette holder, huge false eyelashes and a flapper dress with a headband. She'd have made some gangster a serious moll."

Katrina laughed. "My mother is as down to earth as they come. She's a lot like Mandy. I don't think she had the first clue of what to do with a daughter like me."

The esthetician dried Niki's feet and deftly rubbed in some lotion.

"I bet she baked cookies," Niki guessed.

"She makes every kind imaginable, oatmeal, chocolate chip, peanut butter, and something called monster cookies that I swear have whipped cream in the middle."

"We had standing reservations at—" Niki caught herself. She'd nearly named an iconic New York City restaurant. "Many fine restaurants," she finished.

"You ate out a lot?"

"All the time. Mom didn't cook."

"Not at all?"

"Occasionally, she managed toast."

"You had nothing but toast for breakfast? How did you concentrate at school?"

Niki couldn't help but smile once more at the thought of school. "We traveled a lot," she told Katrina. "Paris, Moscow, Rio. Technically, I was registered at the Melbourne Academy, but they're pretty flexible. I mostly learned on my own, or from tutors. Luckily, I was a quick study. So I easily passed most exams."

Katrina was looking at her oddly.

Sure, Niki knew it was a strange childhood. But Gabriella was restless. She hated to stay too long in one place. Every school year, she promised Niki it would be different. But if they made it through the end of September in their penthouse, it was a banner achievement.

"I thought the Melbourne Academy was in New York," said Katrina.

Niki's thoughts stumbled again. "There must be more than one of them."

"Really?"

For a wild moment, Niki wanted to tell Katrina the whole truth, let the chips fall where they may and get rid of the lump that had lodged itself permanently in her stomach.

"Which color would you like?" the esthetician asked Niki. "Red, violet and copper are our most popular. Or you can choose from the Shimmer Collection or Premier."

Niki looked to the young woman sitting near her feet.

Katrina jumped in. "She wants peach pulse, with gold glitter tips."

"I do?"

"Trust me, you do."

Niki pictured her open toed shoes, the dress, the jewelry. Katrina's suggestion sounded fabulous.

"You're very good at this," she told her.

Katrina grinned. "Purple sky for me." She cocked her head to Niki. "That's Reed's favorite."

For a moment, Niki couldn't help but feel envious of Katrina. She'd love to end this evening in the arms of a boyfriend, lounging together in bed, maybe in a bubble bath, sipping a final glass of champagne while streaks of dawn brightened the sky. It had been a long time since she'd had a truly romantic night out.

Her brain moved to Sawyer, and his amazing kisses. He'd be a wonderful lover. He had to be. She remembered how great his body looked at the river. Though she couldn't exactly picture him in a bubble bath.

"Travis is going to love your outfit," Katrina put in.

Right. Travis. Niki had completely forgotten about Travis.

"Tomboy," Katrina said, shaking her head. "Man, is he in for a surprise."

Niki returned Katrina's smile. It was fun to dress up and look sophisticated again. But she couldn't quash the feeling of disappointment that Sawyer wouldn't be there to see it.

* * *

Sawyer could not get Niki out of his mind. He'd lain awake two nights running, reliving the feel of her slick, wet body pressed up against his. When he thought about her kisses, his body ratcheted up with lust, urging him to track her down and do whatever it took to get her into his bed.

Outside the Lyndon City arena, the cavernous building pulsed with the sounds of a country band and the whoops of hundreds of people enjoying the rodeo dance. He steeled himself against seeing her again. He had to keep his mind clear, or he wouldn't be able to do his job.

"Good luck finding her in all this," said Dylan as they made their way through the doorway and across the foyer.

Sawyer pulled out his wallet and handed a fresh-faced, female door volunteer a twenty.

She stamped his hand with a blue, long-horn head. "Welcome to the Buckaroo Ball."

Sawyer couldn't help but grin at the combination of the name, the stamp, the music and the overall ambiance.

"Not your usual crowd?" Dylan guessed as he handed over his own twenty-dollar bill.

Sawyer surveyed the hundreds of dancers, men in everything from suits and string ties to faded blue jeans and scuffed boots. Most wore Stetsons, and many twirled their partners around in square-dance formation.

There were women in gingham and crinolines, wide skirts that flared out as they whirled. Others wore blue jeans and ponytails. While some were decked out in cocktail dresses and jewelry that could have easily fit in at the Ritz.

"What makes you think I prefer my usual crowd?" he asked Dylan. "This looks like fun."

Sawyer had gone with a pair of blue jeans, a white, Western shirt, and a black blazer, topping the outfit with a white, curved-brim Stetson. As they moved into the crowd, he and Dylan received friendly glances from a number of women. A

perky brunette in a fitted, white, off-the-shoulder, full-skirted
dress gave Dylan a long, alluring gaze.

"I'm having fun already," said Dylan.

"She thinks you're a bronc rider," Sawyer warned.

"I am a bronc rider, and a steer roper and—"

The woman's mouth curved into a broad, sparkling smile.

"Catch you later," Dylan said to Sawyer, tipping his hat to
the woman and offering his arm for a dance.

Letting his grin fade away, Sawyer began moving methodi-
cally through the crowd, scanning as he made his way in the
general direction of a bar. His gaze passed over the back of a
sexy woman in a glimmering gold dress that dipped low and
hugged her rear end. He felt a jolt to his solar plexus.

He paused, staring at her.

She turned, and he saw her profile. It was Niki.

She was speaking with a man, laughing at something he
had said. She held a glass of white wine in one hand, her fin-
gernails shimmering against the pale liquid. Her glasses were
gone. Her makeup was perfect, and her hair was fluffed and
curled, looking beautifully feminine, emphasizing her delicate features.

She looked over at him and their gazes met. A shower of
sparks seemed to flash through his body, making him nearly
burn, before they rushed away, leaving longing in their wake.
Now, *this* was the Niki he'd expected when he first came to
Colorado.

He took an automatic step toward her, while her companion
stopped talking, looking confused. Then the man followed her
line of sight and saw Sawyer baring down. His eyes narrowed.

"Hello, Nellie," Sawyer opened. "You look lovely tonight."

"John Reynolds," the man beside her announced as he stuck
out his hand. It was a challenge more than a greeting.

"Sawyer Smith," Sawyer returned, shaking, taking his eyes
off Niki for only the barest of seconds. "Pleased to meet you."

John Reynolds glanced from Sawyer to Niki. "You know
this guy?"

"He's my neighbor," she answered, her own gaze still resting on Sawyer.

Then she seemed to catch herself, and she returned her attention to John. "He just bought the Raklin Place, across from Reed and Caleb."

"Oh, new in town," John observed, his arms crossing over his broad chest.

He wore a blue plaid shirt, the sleeves rolled up, and a new pair of blue jeans. His face was clean shaven, and his hair was trimmed neat. But there was something keenly predatory and proprietary in his eyes. His hands were beefy and strong, liberally covered in calluses.

The thought of him touching Niki sent Sawyer's blood pressure climbing. Every instinct he possessed told him to get her away from this guy.

"New in town," Sawyer acknowledged.

He returned his attention to Niki, vaguely annoyed now that she'd dressed to the nines. Didn't she know what kind of attention she'd attract?

"Nellie," came a new voice, and Travis Jacobs stepped up, beaming at her. "I believe you promised me a dance."

And, just like that, Niki was swept onto the dance floor, and Sawyer was left standing next to John.

"I realize you're new in town," said John. "But I'm going to warn you—"

"That Nellie is taken?" Sawyer arched a brow, watching her smile in Travis's arms. At the moment, he was jealous of Travis, not John.

"I have no desire to fight you," John warned.

Sawyer nodded to Niki and Travis on the dance floor. "It doesn't look like I'm the one you'll have to fight." Though Sawyer felt like taking on Travis himself all of a sudden.

Why did Niki look so relaxed and happy with Travis Jacobs? And why were they suddenly a thing? Both of them had been at the construction barbecue. And they'd both been at the river swim. Travis hadn't shown any interest in Niki then, nor she in him.

"They're practically family," said John, but his gaze narrowed on Travis.

The music crested toward the end of the song, and Sawyer asked himself why he was wasting any more time talking to John. He set a course for Niki, and stepped up, just as the music faded.

"Dance?" he asked her, ignoring the glare Travis sent his way.

Niki shot a quick, questioning glance to Travis, but then nodded her agreement to Sawyer.

He drew her into his arms. Thankfully, the next tune was slow, and he had an excuse to pull her in close. Her compact curves moved up against him, thighs touching his, breasts brushing his chest. If he looked down, he could see the delightful curve of her cleavage, creamy breasts draped in shimmering gold.

"John seems to like you," Sawyer opened, seeking information.

She tipped her chin, looking up at him, her movements sinuously matching his own. "He's a nice guy."

"Nice, as in you'd like to share an iced tea at the kitchen table? Or nice as in you'd like to share a moonlight walk by the lake?"

"Aren't you nosey."

"I thought you might like to know that he's thinking about the moonlight walk, and more."

"Have I done something to make you think I'm stupid?"

Sawyer was beginning to think she was brilliant, cunningly and deviously brilliant. She'd co-opted half of Lyndon Valley by blinking her big green eyes and pouting those sexy, red lips. And right now, she had three different men vying for her.

"You're not wearing glasses," he said instead of answering.

"Contacts."

"They look nice. You look nice. In fact, you look stunningly gorgeous." For some reason, Sawyer's mouth kept going when his brain told him to shut up.

"You are a gentleman, Sawyer Smith."

"Are you a lady, Nellie Cooper?"

She drew back, frowning. "I take it back. You're a cad."

"A *cad?* You've been hanging around Colorado too long."

"What's that supposed to mean?"

Sawyer regrouped. "*Cad* is not exactly a Boston term."

"You're an expert on Boston? You're from Montana."

"I've also been to Boston, and I've been overseas."

"Really? Where?"

"Off the East Coast of Africa. In the Mediterranean. Through the Suez Canal. Wherever there was trouble or potential trouble."

"Have you seen a lot of the world?" she asked, the edge gone from her tone, replaced by what seemed to be genuine curiosity.

"I have. Not all of it fun."

"I've been to Paris and London, Rome and Monte Carlo."

"Now those places are the fun." Sawyer had certainly heard about Gabriella's glamorous lifestyle. His research told him that she'd taken Niki to dozens of major cities, showed her most of the seven wonders.

"I saw a lot of it from a hotel room with a nanny."

"You were young?" he asked, already knowing the answer. Niki's world travels had started before she could walk.

"I'm still young," she joked.

"Twenty-one's not that young." He felt a strange need to remind himself she was an adult. Sure, there were nine years between them, but twenty-one to his thirty wasn't a gap worth worrying about.

Then he caught himself. Where the hell were those thoughts going? He was investigating her, not dating her. The age difference between them was irrelevant.

"How did you know I was twenty-one?" she asked.

He missed a beat in the dance. "Somebody mentioned it. I think maybe it was at the barbecue."

"Do I look that young?" she seemed concerned.

"You look timeless, Nellie. Beautifully timeless."

She smiled, and a shot of desire gripped his chest. "You're back to being a gentleman again."

"That's only because you don't know what I'm thinking." Despite his resolve, he was thinking he'd like to tear off her clothes, bruise that gorgeous mouth with his kisses, and make hard, passionate love to her until neither of them could see straight.

She blinked, and something shifted in the depths of her eyes. Her tone went husky. "What are you thinking?"

His fingertips tightened convulsively at the small of her back, and the tips of her breasts seemed to tease his chest provocatively. He held her gaze. "You don't want to be asking me that."

"I just did."

"I am fire, Nellie Cooper. And you are definitely playing with it."

Someone tapped Sawyer on the shoulder.

It was John, and his tone was icy. "I believe the next dance is mine."

Sawyer's hold automatically tightened on Niki. Any other time, any other place, he wouldn't give her up. But he couldn't do anything stupid right now. He couldn't bring attention to himself. And he had to tread carefully where this relationship was concerned. He needed Niki's trust, her confidence. He needed her to like him, but he needed to keep his distance, as well.

"Sure," he said to John, forcing himself to release her and step away.

"Thank you," he said to Niki, then he clenched his jaw and turned his back, pacing his way off the dance floor.

As Niki danced with John, she thought about Sawyer's question. John was definitely an iced-tea-at-the-kitchen-table kind of guy. She couldn't imagine a moonlight stroll with him. And she sure couldn't imagine anything more.

The reason she could so easily tell the difference, was that she could imagine all of those things with Sawyer. She could imagine anything and everything with Sawyer. Which was extremely dangerous. At the moment, she wasn't in a position to embark on anything more than iced tea in the kitchen with any man in Colorado.

At the end of her dance with John, Travis cut in.

"Popular woman tonight," he told her, leading her into a spin and then back into his arms.

The music had grown livelier, and couples were having fun with the tunes.

"I think there's an uneven ratio of men to women," she observed.

"I thought it was the gold dress." He swung her around in a circle.

"You know Katrina took me for a makeover."

"I do."

"And," Niki hesitated. "You know she, uh, well..."

"My baby sister is as transparent as they come." Travis smiled. "I'm guessing she woke up yesterday and realized we were both single."

"I tried to talk her out of it."

Travis twirled Niki out, then reeled her back. He really was a fun dancer, more skilled than John, less intense than Sawyer. She found herself enjoying the music more and more.

"I'm sure you did," he told her, wrapping his arm around her waist again. "And did she listen?"

"Not even for a second."

"So, what do you say, Nellie. You want to give it a try between us?"

Niki stumbled, her expression sobered.

But Travis laughed, and she noted there was a mischievous twinkle in his eyes. He drew her close, leaning down to her ear.

"The way I see it, Nellie. If there was a spark between us,

we'd have noticed before now. Katrina's not-so-secret plan notwithstanding, I don't need a sexy dress and a fancy hairdo to notice a woman. If I was the one, you'd have noticed me covered in manure. And, if you were the one, I'd have noticed you in sackcloth."

Niki drew back. "Do you truly believe that?"

"I truly do."

For Niki, it was the first time Travis had differentiated himself from the general crowd of Terrell and Jacobs ranch workers and family members. She felt as though she was meeting him for the first time.

"Do you think we could like each other enough to be friends?" she found herself asking.

"I think we could like each other just fine. I already like you, Nellie. And, hey." He drew back and gave her a slow once-over. "I could sleep with you at the drop of a hat."

She couldn't help but grin at his audacity.

"But I don't see us living happily ever after."

"Neither do I," she admitted.

He smoothed back her hair. "And, I could be wrong, but I think two marriages between the Jacobs and Terrell families are plenty. Any more, we might be tempting fate."

Niki let loose with a loud laugh. "You went from Katrina dressing me up, to the two of us possibly walking down the aisle, in the space of an hour and a half?"

"I believe in cutting to the chase."

"You certainly do."

The song began to draw to a close.

"Travis?"

"Yeah?"

"When you do fall for someone? Let me say right off that she's going to be a very lucky woman. But, my advice? You might want to wait a day or two before popping the question."

It was Travis's turn to laugh. "I'll try to restrain myself."

Niki reached up to squeeze his hand where it rested on her shoulder. "Thanks for the dance, Travis."

"You do know Katrina's been watching us with baited breath the entire time."

Niki closed her eyes for a long second. "What should we tell her?"

He shrugged. "I'm not going to tell her anything. Let her stay curious for a while. It'll serve her right."

"Is that how brothers treat their sisters?"

"Absolutely, Nellie. We teased them half to death. And I feel like you're my new sister."

She struggled not to grin. "You're frightening me now."

"Don't worry, it's not all bad having me as a brother."

The song came to a close, and Travis escorted her off the floor. Niki was happy to take a break.

Very quickly, she spotted Sawyer. He was sitting at one of the many bars that dotted the perimeter of the arena, sipping a bottle of beer. She decided she needed to set things on the right course between them. He had a point. She was playing with fire, and their flirtation had to come to an end.

She crossed to him, hopping up on the seat next to him.

"Looked like fun," he drawled, an edge to his voice.

"What looked like fun?" Then she turned to the bartender. "Chardonnay, please."

"That dance."

"Which dance?" She'd just danced with Sawyer, then John, then Travis.

"Talking, laughing, touching. I thought Travis was going to kiss you right out there in front of everyone."

The light went on inside Niki's brain. Sawyer had completely misunderstood the body language between her and Travis. She opened her mouth to correct him, but then stopped herself.

If Sawyer thought she was interested in Travis, maybe he'd back off of flirting with her. She accepted the drink from the waiter. Before she could dig out some money, Sawyer was tossing a bill on the bar.

"Thank you," she told him.

"No problem." He took a swig of his beer.

"Travis is a very nice man," she added.

Sawyer stared at the crowd. "I take it John doesn't have a chance?"

She ran her finger along the condensation from the cold glass. "John's iced tea in the kitchen."

"And Travis is a midnight stroll by the lake."

She shrugged, for some reason not wanting to outright lie to Sawyer.

"And more?" Sawyer asked.

She swiveled to face him. "That's a very rude question."

"I've given up being a gentleman."

"Were you ever a gentleman?"

He angled his body toward her, and she caught a whiff of his scent. It was enticing and intriguing. It cut through the wood and leather, the beer and champagne. It shot straight through her brain, and her entire body clenched with desire for him.

His tone went low and gravelly. "I can fake being a gentleman, Nellie. But don't let me fool you. Deep down, I'm as devious as they come."

She kept her tone light, even though her blood was beginning to sing with arousal. Her lips tingled and a bead of sweat gathered between her breasts. "I'm surprised you would give that away about yourself."

"So am I."

Silence grew between them. The music from the band seemed to fade, and the stomping of boots on the dance floor muted. His very gaze reached out and swirled around her, bands of energy pulling her toward him.

"What am I, Nellie?" His fingertips came to rest on her bare knee, and she knew exactly what he was asking.

She knew she should refuse to answer, but she couldn't stop herself. "You're the guy who skips the iced tea, skips the moonlight stroll and invites a girl straight to the hayloft."

A half smile quirked at the corner of his mouth. "You're a smart woman, Nellie Cooper."

"I'm smart enough to know when to run away."

"Are you running away now?"

She slid from the barstool, determined to do the smart thing. She nodded, but then forced out the words. "Travis is a good man."

Five

Sawyer reached for Niki's hand, grasping it just in time to stop her from walking away. He was making a colossal mess of everything. He was supposed to be gaining her trust, not scaring her off with talk of flings in haylofts.

"What?" she asked.

"I'm sorry," he began. "I didn't mean to—"

The band went suddenly silent, and the arena plunged into darkness. An instantaneous whoop went up from the cowboys, and Sawyer reflexively pulled Niki to him, sheltering her in the dark.

Lightning flashed through the open doorways at the far end of the arena, and thunder rumbled its way through the big building.

"You okay?" he asked her, keeping his arms solidly around her cradling her between his bent knees. He heard a glass break nearby, and someone bumped against his shoulder. He turned his body, putting her between him and the bar.

Lightning flashed again, and thunder cracked directly above them.

"Last summer, they had a storm that blew down half the trees in Lyndon Valley," she told him. "It closed the airport for three days."

"Exciting place, Colorado," Sawyer replied.

Voices around them rose and fell. Most people seemed to be taking the blackout in stride. He could see cell phones coming out as light sources all around them.

He lowered his voice. "I'm not looking for a fling."

"Yeah, well, you're not getting one. So, that's good."

He couldn't quite peg the tone of her voice. Was she joking with him? "I don't know why I said I was devious. I've never invited a girl to a hayloft."

"Not even once?" she teased.

"Not an unwilling one," he joked back. Then he sobered. "I feel like we got off on the wrong foot." He felt his way along her arm to her hand, taking it gently in his to shake. "Let's try again. Hi, I'm Sawyer Smith, your new neighbor, here to be friendly and assist you in any way I can."

"Nellie Cooper." She shook his hand, and there was a smile in her voice. "Single, and definitely not looking."

He couldn't help but grin at that. "Not looking for what?"

"A man. A relationship. Anything more than a friend." She shifted closer in the intimacy of the darkness. "My life is complicated right now."

"Complicated how?" He had to concentrate on keeping his hands to himself. Her vanilla-scented shampoo teased his senses, and she had the sexiest voice, especially when it was low, husky with a touch of whisper.

"I've just found my brothers. I'm getting my feet under me in Colorado."

"I can respect that. I'm getting my feet under me, too."

"I guess you are," she agreed. "So, why did you leave the navy?"

"My family," he allowed. "They were…worried about me."

"Your mother?"

"My mother passed away several years ago. And my father was killed shortly after. But I have a large extended family. We're quite close."

"They're in Montana?"

"Mostly," he hedged.

She was silent for a moment. A few flashlights had gone on around them, and the bartender lit a couple of candles at the far end of the bar.

"So, you lost your mother, too," Niki said.

"I did."

"How old were you?"

"Twenty-two. I joined the navy right after."

"Did it hurt for long?"

He gave in to the urge to rub his hand over the small of her back. "It gets better. You must miss yours a lot."

"I do." Another silence. "She wasn't exactly a conventional mother."

"How so?" Sawyer struggled to contain his eagerness. This was exactly the kind of conversation he'd been hoping to have.

The bartender banged something beside them, causing Niki to still. Sawyer held his breath.

But then the man moved on, obviously packing up the liquor.

"She was an orphan," said Niki. "Her parents died in a car accident when she was eleven."

Sawyer hadn't known that. Interesting that it wasn't something he'd come across in his research.

"She was in and out of a few foster homes. She ran away from the last one when she was fifteen, taking care of herself after that. She called it 'living by her wits.' Sometimes it meant sleeping with wealthy men. Not that they paid her for sex."

"I didn't assume—"

"They usually gave her a place to stay. You know, downtown apartments while their families lived in the suburbs. Things like that. They bought her gifts, gave her advice. She told me she listened carefully to everything they said, overheard hundreds of telephone conversations, and eventually discovered the stock market."

Sawyer found himself grudgingly admiring Gabriella.

"She studied hard and learned how to put the pieces together. Eventually, she had enough money to take care of herself. But she still kept up the affairs. I think she felt safer with men who could never claim her as their own."

Niki fell to silence. "I don't know why I'm telling you all this."

Neither did Sawyer. He was shocked at her openness. Not that she'd revealed her mother's name. And she did assume he thought she was from Boston.

"Oh, I remember," said Niki. "I had an unconventional childhood. That was my point. Ga— My mother and I were more like sisters or friends. She was only eighteen when she had me, and nobody had ever taught her how to be a mother, so she assumed what she found fun, I would find fun. And once she had money, we played our way from Rio to the South of France."

"How did you go to school?"

Niki laughed. "Off and on. Luckily, I was smart, and I caught up easily."

"I'm convinced you're intelligent," Sawyer told her honestly. "What happened to the money?"

"What do you mean?"

He chose his words carefully. "You're living with your brothers. I assume that means that money's gone?" It would also give her a strong motive for blackmailing the people in the diary.

"The money's not gone," she told him softly.

The storm continued to rumble above them. Aided by their cell phones and the occasional flashlight, people were making their way toward the exit. The bartender had loaded up a cart of supplies and was pushing them away.

"Yet, you're here," Sawyer said to Niki. His eyes had adjusted to the darkness, but she was still a dim outline in front of him.

"I'm here to meet my brothers."

"Are you staying?"

A soft sigh escaped from her lips, and she rested her hand on his thigh. "Some days, I wish I could."

There were so many things he wanted to ask her, so many things he didn't dare.

He put his hand on top of hers. "Where are you sleeping tonight?"

As soon as the words were out, he could have kicked himself. "I'm sorry. I didn't mean—I wasn't asking—I wasn't making you an offer. Not that I wouldn't make you an offer." Sawyer didn't know what was the matter with him. He didn't ramble like this. He simply didn't.

She hadn't responded.

"I'm not trying to flirt," he assured her. "But it does seem to be some kind of a knee-jerk reaction when it comes to you."

Her finger went across his lips. "You should probably stop talking."

"Yeah."

"I'm sleeping at the Mayor's mansion. Seth Jacobs is Katrina's oldest brother."

Sawyer barely heard the words. Niki's index finger was soft and warm across his lips, and it was all he could do not to kiss it, draw it into his mouth, curl his tongue around it.

His hand wrapped around her waist. He widened his knees, drawing her closer still. The rain pounded on the metal roof, even as stillness closed in around them. They were all alone in the corner of the building.

He kissed her finger.

She sucked in a breath, but didn't pull it away.

He touched it with the tip of his tongue, and she drew a line along his lower lip.

Sawyer's heart rate kicked up, his blood pulsing heat into every inch of his body. With his palm, he stroked along her shoulder, up the curve of her neck, cradling her head, anchoring her while he came to his feet and dipped his head toward her.

His lips met hers, hot, soft and ready. Their tongues tangled, before he fully captured her mouth.

One arm anchored her, while the other slipped up into her hair. She wound her arms around his neck, tipping her head, her breasts pressing hard against his chest. His hand spanned her waist, finding the curve of her hipbone, moving upward. Unable to resist, he cupped her breast.

A moan emerged from deep in her chest, and his passion jackknifed. He slid his hand downward, following the curve of her bottom, to the hem of her dress, touching the soft skin of her thigh. Her arms tightened around his neck, and she deepened the kiss, molding herself to him.

He marshaled his strength, broke their kiss, looking around to make sure they were still all alone. Thunder echoed through the cavernous building. Other voices sounded far, far away.

"You're beautiful," he growled low. "So incredibly, amazingly exquisite."

His hand slipped beneath her hemline, sliding up to the silk of her tiny panties.

She groaned.

He kissed her deeper.

Thunder rumbled, lightning brightening the room.

She wrenched back. "We can't."

"I'm sorry," he quickly apologized, appalled that he'd taken the kiss so far, and in a public place.

"I think I must be drunk."

"We got carried away," he allowed. He couldn't quite bring himself to let her go, holding her loosely, promising himself he wouldn't make another move.

After all the lectures he'd given himself, and the rational reasons to keep his distance from her, he'd made out with her in a dark corner? What was he, eighteen?

"Can we forget this ever happened?" she asked in a small voice.

"We can try." He knew he wouldn't be forgetting about it anytime soon.

"Sawyer."

"Fine." He scooped her up into his arms.

"Hey!"

"It's forgotten."

"What are you *doing?*"

"There's broken glass all over the floor. I don't want you to get hurt."

"I won't get hurt," she huffed.

"Now that's just ridiculous. How do I get you to the Mayor's house?"

Still carried securely in Sawyer's arms, Niki stared out from under the arena awning at the whipping wind and the crashing rain. One of his arms cradled her shoulders, the other supported her thighs, positioned to ensure her dress kept her appropriately covered.

"Wow," the word whooshed out of his mouth. "Now that's a storm."

Few people remained on the sidewalk, and the parking lot was quickly emptying, SUVs and pickup trucks splashing through large puddles, while their headlights broke through the thick darkness of the blacked-out night.

"Were you supposed to meet the Terrells somewhere?" Sawyer asked.

"Katrina and I took a cab to get here, but we didn't have any specific plans for the ride home."

Sawyer set her gently down on her feet on the damp concrete. The rain was blowing all around them, whipping them with the occasional spray of cold mist.

He shrugged out of his jacket, draping it around her shoulders, at the same time extracting his cell phone.

"Thanks." She pushed her arms into the big sleeves. The satin lining was still warm from his body.

Sawyer tried a number and listened for a few moments. He drew the phone from his ear and tried something else.

"Lines are jammed up," he said to Niki.

She wasn't surprised to hear that. The blackout probably affected the service, and everybody in town must be calling each other right now. "Can I try Katrina?"

He handed her the phone.

Niki pressed the buttons for Katrina's number. "It's ringing," she said to Sawyer.

"Hello?" came Katrina's voice, muffled by the noise of the storm. The lightning flashes crackled on the signal.

"It's Niki."

"Oh, thank goodness. Where are you? Are you all right?"

"I'm fine. I'm at the entrance to the arena. With Sawyer."

There was a pause. "You're not with Travis?"

"No. I danced with Travis. But then we got separated." Travis had been such a good sport about the matchmaking that Niki didn't want to confess they were only going to be friends just yet and spoil his fun.

Sawyer's expression soured ever so slightly.

"Did you make it to Seth's?" she asked Katrina.

"We just got here. Trees are coming down all over the place. I can send the driver back for you."

"Should she send the driver back for us?" Niki asked Sawyer.

"Tell her I'll drop you off. I've got my pickup."

"Sawyer's got a pickup," she said to Katrina. "He can drop me off. Are you worried about Travis?"

"Travis can take care of himself. I'm worried about you."

"I'm warm and dry," said Niki, pulling Sawyer's jacket more fully around her.

"You won't stay that way for long," Katrina warned.

"I'll live."

"There'll be cookies and cocoa when you get here."

"Sounds yummy. Thanks."

"See you soon."

Niki rang off and handed the phone back to Sawyer. "Far to your truck?" she asked.

"It's on the creek side of the parking lot. Quite a ways over. I'll go and get it."

She took in the lines of traffic snaking their way in all directions in the parking lot. "It'll take you a long time to backtrack." She looked up at him. "I think I'd rather be sitting in a warm truck than standing here waiting in the wind."

He hesitated, but then agreed with a nod. A second later, she was hoisted back up into his arms.

"I can walk," she protested.

But he was moving forward. "Didn't we already have this argument?"

"There's no broken glass out here."

"We don't know that for sure. And the puddles are deep. And the parking lot is muddy. And I don't want you to slow me down."

They came out from under the shelter, and fat raindrops pelted them. Niki reflexively turned her face into Sawyer's chest. He increased his pace.

"I must be heavy. I'm sorry." She felt obligated to apologize.

He chuckled. "I've carried bigger loads in worse conditions."

"I'm a *load?*" Wasn't that flattering.

"An easy load. If it makes you feel any better, you're a lot prettier than a mooring line, and nothing's pitching beneath my feet."

"Excuse me?"

"Ever been on board a frigate in thirty-foot seas?"

"I've been on a cruise ship."

"In a first-class cabin?"

"Usually, a high-end suite," she admitted. "But we had some rough water."

He took long strides around the numerous puddles that had

formed on the gravel parking lot. "I'm sure it's pretty much the same thing."

"You're mocking me."

"I'm trying to reassure you. You're not that heavy, and you're a lot more fun to carry than my usual cargo."

"Oh, well, thank you."

"You're welcome. Here we are." He came to a halt, popping open the passenger door on a shiny, blue pickup. He deposited her on the bench seat.

She put a hand on his arm. "Seriously, Sawyer, thank you."

He smiled, rainwater dampening his face and dripping from his hat brim. "Seriously, Nellie, you're welcome."

He closed the door, sloshing his way around to the driver's seat, where he hopped in and slammed the door against the rain outside. He tossed his hat into the backseat, then he extracted the keys from his jeans pocket and shoved one into the ignition.

He turned it.

Nothing happened.

He turned it again, but there was dead silence.

"Battery?" Niki speculated.

"Seems unlikely," he frowned.

"Did you leave your headlights on?"

"It was still light out when I got here."

Just then, a lightning flash cracked across the sky, illuminating the hood in front of them, revealing a black streak from the windshield to the hood ornament. The paint was bubbled and peeled to the metal.

"It was struck by lightning?" Niki could barely believe it.

"Must have fried the electrical," said Sawyer, sitting back in his seat.

"That can't be good."

"It's not good."

She glanced out the windows. "Are we safe here?"

He craned his neck, looking up at the dark sky. "The storm's moving on. And, really, what are the mathematical odds?"

"Of lightning striking twice in the same place? I've heard they're higher than you might think."

"Are you afraid?"

"Not really," Niki answered honestly.

He was right. The storm did seem to be moving on. And she had no desire to brave the rain again to get back inside the arena.

Sawyer extracted his cell phone, trying a few numbers, but failing to connect.

Then he handed it to Niki. "You seem to have better luck than me."

She dialed Katrina, but didn't get through. She wasn't even getting a dial tone anymore.

She handed back the phone. "What now?"

He took it. "We can walk back or wait here. Up to you."

She squinted out at the storm. "I don't have any desire to go back out there."

"Then we wait. The chaos will calm down eventually. The phone lines will free up, and we can call a cab, or get through to Dylan or Katrina." He reached behind them to the jump seat in the back, rattling something out of a plastic bag.

"Horse blanket," he told her, bringing it forward. "But it's brand-new and pure wool."

As he unwrapped it from the packaging, he urged her to move closer. She scooted to the middle of the bench seat.

The plaid blanket was oddly shaped and slightly scratchy to her skin. But it was big enough to share, and the minute it was over them, she started to warm up.

"Nice." She sighed.

"Nice," he agreed. He stretched his arm across the back of the seat, and she had to resist the comfortable-looking spot he'd inadvertently created.

"I guess this wasn't how you expected the evening to end," he ventured.

"It wasn't even in the top ten."

"Tell me more about Boston."

Niki went on alert. She'd been to Boston a few times in her life, but she wasn't prepared for an in-depth discussion of the city. "Why?"

"I find your childhood interesting," Sawyer answered easily. "I'd like to hear more."

"Tell me about yours," Niki countered. "What was life like in Montana?"

"Fair enough," he agreed. "Well, let me see. You haven't met Dylan yet, but you will. He's the ranch manager at my place. We were good friends growing up on the ranch in Montana. We were a little wild, a little out of control."

"A bad boy?" Niki found herself asking, at the same time trying to convince herself that she didn't find it sexy.

"I guess you could call it that. Most Saturday nights, we commandeered both liquor and transportation from the ranch. Picked up girls. Got into fights."

"With each other?"

"Huh?"

"Did you fight with each other?"

"No. Never. We mostly fought with the boyfriends of the girls we picked up."

"You poached the girlfriends of other boys?"

"Sure. The town boys didn't like the ranch boys, and vice versa. But the girls like the boys with the cars."

She shifted so that she could see the outline of his expression in the darkness. "Are you morally challenged?"

He didn't miss a beat. "Most would say yes."

"You're a reprobate."

"And a cad."

"And—"

"Shhh," he warned her.

"What?"

"Listen."

A low rumbling sound came from the distance. It seemed to grow closer. It got louder. The truck began to vibrate.

Sawyer swore, bracing his feet against the floorboard and yanking Niki into his arms.

"Creek's overflowed," he announced. "That's a flash flood."

The truck lurched, moving several feet to the side. Objects banged one after the other into the driver's door and the side of the box.

Niki stifled a scream, burying her face in Sawyer's chest. Her hands automatically fisted around his shirt, hanging on tight against the jarring movement.

The truck lifted, it swung around, the force of the water pushing it backward, debris continuing to rattle and bang against it.

"Hang on," he warned.

"Are we going to die?" she dared to ask.

"It seems unlikely," he responded.

"I'd rather you'd said no."

"No." He gathered her closer.

"Are you sure?"

"Positive."

Despite her fear, she couldn't help but grin at that. "You're a liar."

"I am, indeed. But, the creek's not that deep. I don't think we'll sink, and I don't think we'll drown. So far, we haven't flipped over. So, that's good."

"You're analyzing our situation, calculating the odds of outcomes."

"Sure."

"I'm blindly freaking out here."

His chest rumbled as he chuckled. The truck jerked to a stop as it obviously hit something. Then it shifted sideways, with a screech of wrenching metal.

"I don't think the truck is going to survive," Sawyer observed.

The turn happened in slow motion, until the passenger door slammed into a tree, bringing everything to a halt. Water was still washing around them from the driver's side, and objects were clanking against the metal.

"If it gets as high as the glass," said Sawyer, easing them toward the passenger side of the vehicle. "I'll kick out the back window, and we can climb that tree."

Niki swallowed, her throat dry as sandpaper. "Are you serious?"

"I'm serious."

"I thought you said we weren't going to drown."

"We're not."

"We're going to kick out a window and climb a tree?"

"Only if we have to."

"Sawyer," she pleaded.

"What? I'm not making this up to annoy you. I'm suggesting our best options."

"I don't like this."

"Well, I'm not that thrilled about it, either. Driftwood is pounding the life out of my brand-new truck."

"I'm sorry about that," she allowed.

"It's not your fault."

"I'm still sorry your truck's being destroyed."

"It doesn't matter."

"Sawyer?"

"Yeah?"

"There's water leaking in."

"I know."

"I feel like we should say or do something momentous."

Maybe she should confess her sins, tell him her secrets. Did she want to go to her grave having lied to *everyone* in Lyndon Valley?

Sawyer wasn't exactly the object of her duplicity, but telling him would be something, right? She couldn't confess to her brothers or her sisters-in-law right now. If Sawyer survived, and she didn't, he could tell her newfound family the truth. She mustered her courage.

"Sawyer?"

"Shh. Listen."

"What?"

"Sirens. I can see the lights. The fire department is on its way."

Within minutes, her world became a jumble of flashing lights and shouting voices. Sawyer packed her into a harness, and the firemen towed her to safety. They rescued Sawyer next, and soon she was in the back of a fire-department truck, wrapped in a soft blanket.

Then she was deposited at the Mayor's mansion, where Katrina fussed, and Reed barked orders, and she was quickly dry and changed and being ushered into an armchair in the great room of the historic building.

Niki had never felt like this before, surrounded by family, surrounded by capable people who genuinely seemed to care about her welfare. She was dressed in a pair of loose, grey sweatpants and a baggy blue T-shirt. Seth, the mayor and Katrina's oldest brother, had brought her a cup of cocoa, and someone made sure there was a tray of cookies on the table beside her.

The fire department had given Sawyer a ride to his hotel. But Reed was hovering over her now. It seemed as if he was searching for some way to help.

"Thank you," Niki told him sincerely.

"I should have come after you right away," said Reed, crouching on one knee next to her chair. "Why didn't you tell us you needed help?"

"We were fine when I talked to Katrina. We thought the truck would start and we'd drive home like everybody else."

"It's a mess out there," said Reed. "I should have expected something like this."

Katrina moved closer and put a hand on Reed's shoulder. "She's fine, sweetheart. She's fine."

"No thanks to me."

"You can help with the cleanup tomorrow," Katrina told him.

Her words seemed to appease Reed, who stood again.

"Another cookie?" asked Katrina.

"I'm stuffed," said Niki. She glanced around the room, finding only Reed, Seth and Katrina left.

This was her moment. This was her chance. She mustered her courage and principles, knowing there was no backing away. "I need to talk to you guys, if that's okay."

Katrina took her hand. "Please tell me you're not going back to Boston. It's not always like this in Lyndon Valley, I promise."

"It's not that."

Well, maybe not that. Once Niki shared what she had to say, she might very well be packing up and heading for Boston or Alaska, or maybe even Canada.

She was struck with a moment of terrible doubt. Should she really tell them tonight? Would they toss her out into the storm? And, if they felt morally obligated to let her stay here for the night, how awkward would it be at breakfast?

Once again, Gabriella's voice was inside her head, urging her to put it off. The truth would still be the truth in the morning. And, in the morning, if she needed to make a clean getaway, she could do it. It would be colossally foolish to anger everyone tonight when there was no place for her to go.

"Nellie?" Katrina prompted. "Is something wrong?"

"Yes," said Niki, steeling her nerve. "Something's very wrong. And I have to tell you about it."

Six

Sawyer was too keyed up to sleep. Though he'd hardly classify the experience a brush with death, he'd hated having to put Niki in that kind of danger. At the same time, he'd loved kissing her, and he'd relished those moments he'd held her so close in his arms. It had been a foolish mistake, losing control like that, one that he didn't dare repeat.

Still, a man could think about it, and a man could relive it. And then a man could get screaming drunk so he'd have a hope in hell of blotting out the memories.

He dumped another minibar bottle of scotch over the ice cubes in his glass.

The suite door swung open, and Dylan walked in. "Wondered if you'd make it back," he began without preamble.

"Almost didn't," said Sawyer. "The creek flooded, and the truck washed away."

"Ouch." Dylan crossed to the bar.

"We're going to need a new truck."

"Anybody hurt?" Dylan asked as he selected a rye whiskey.

Like Sawyer, he tossed a couple of ice cubes into a glass and drained the small bottle.

"Niki was with me."

"Yeah?"

"Back in the bosom of her family now."

Where she belonged, if Sawyer was honest with himself. The more he got to know her, the less he liked what was happening to her.

Dylan swirled the drink in his glass as he moved to the living area. "Learn anything new?"

"Not about the diary." But Sawyer had certainly learned that she was a good kisser, and an incredibly responsive and passionate woman. He also confirmed that he'd give just about anything he had to get her into bed.

"I saw you danced with her."

"I did."

"Rethinking my plan to romance her?"

"Not on purpose."

Dylan took a seat in a leather wingback chair. "Okay, that's intriguing."

Sawyer didn't mean to be intriguing. He meant to mentally beat himself up. "Letting myself get attracted to her is a stupid move."

"So, don't do it."

Sawyer shot him a hard stare.

"There are a lot of hot women in the world, Sawyer. You don't have to sleep with them all."

"I don't want to sleep with them all."

"This would be a good time to start exercising restraint."

Sawyer had to admit, Dylan was right about that. Niki was sexy to the point of peril. It was in her genes. It was how Gabriella had manipulated half of D.C. And he still couldn't completely discount the possibility that Niki was playing him.

"I kissed her," Sawyer admitted.

"No harm in that. Just don't do anything else. Take her on a picnic or something."

"A *picnic?*" What was this, 1950?

"Play the sweet, genteel suitor. Bring her flowers and candy. Sit on the front-porch swing."

"Have you been watching too much vintage television?"

"Convince her you're a nice guy. Romance her, don't seduce her."

Sawyer feared it might be a little late to change tactics.

"Kiss her, but be sure you don't take it any further. That'll get her to start talking," Dylan finished.

"What makes you such an expert?" Sawyer asked.

He hated to admit it, but he was beginning to agree with Dylan. He had to wrap this thing up, and he had to do it quick. His family was at stake, and dating Niki was probably the fastest way to gain her trust. But romancing her, while restraining his instincts to seduce her, was going to be one tough slog.

"Observations on human nature," said Dylan.

"I thought it might be practice." Sawyer couldn't resist.

"Never had a reason to practice restraint," said Dylan. He paused. "Hope I never do."

"But you're quick to volunteer me."

"It's your job," Dylan reminded him. "It's why you're here."

"Fair enough." Sawyer had to be a man about this. He hadn't come to Colorado to satisfy his lust. He was here for his family, to save his uncle's political career. "We'll try it your way."

Niki all but squirmed under three pairs of curious eyes. Her mother's voice inside her brain was loudly condemning. And she desperately wanted to wait until morning to make this confession. But she knew if she let it slide again, she might never tell them the truth.

"What is it?" Katrina asked. She sat down on the sofa near Niki, while both Reed and Seth remained standing.

Niki swallowed. She tried valiantly to ignore the warning that was churning in her stomach and Gabriella's lecture pounding out at the base of her brain.

"I'm not Nellie Cooper," she blurted out.

Gabriella's voice went silent. Probably in shock.

Katrina, Reed and Seth all exchanged confused looks.

"I don't understand," Katrina said.

"I'm not Nellie Cooper." Niki's voice came out softer this time, raspy across her drying throat. "My name is Niki Gerard."

There. It was out. It was done, and she couldn't call it back.

There was a slight quaver in Katrina's voice. "You're not our sister?"

"Oh, no," Niki quickly assured her. "It's not—"

"You *lied* to us?" Reed boomed.

"I... Yes," Niki admitted, braving a look at her brother. "I lied to you all."

Katrina came shakily to her feet, backing a few steps away.

"I'm sorry," Niki quickly offered, her throat going from dry with fear to raw with pain.

"We invited you into our home," Katrina murmured in obvious disbelief.

"We *trusted* you," Reed barked.

"Who are you?" Seth asked, voice milder than Reed's.

"I'm Niki Gerard," Niki repeated.

But Seth shook his head. "*Who* are you? Why would you come here? Why would you do that?"

"I'm your sister," Niki said to Reed. "I'm not from Boston, and my name's not Nellie, but everything else—"

"You're a fraud," Reed spat.

"Wait, Reed," said Seth, staring at Niki with undisguised curiosity.

"Wait for what?" Reed challenged. "For another lie? I don't think so." He turned on his heel and stomped from the room.

Katrina looked distressed and confused. But she quickly followed her husband.

Niki clenched her jaw, determined not to cry. She gripped the arm of the sofa, preparing to rise, hoping her legs would hold her. She wished she could walk straight out the front door.

But her purse was upstairs in one of the bedrooms. She needed that at the very least.

She stood. She wasn't sure how she'd get the rest of her things from the Terrells' ranch, but she'd have to work that out later. Right now, getting herself out of here was as much as she could manage.

"What are you doing?" Seth demanded as she took a step toward the formal staircase.

"I am so sorry," she managed, her voice cracking ever so slightly with the effort. "I need my things."

"Where are you going?"

"Upstairs." She didn't know what she'd do if he threw her directly out the front door.

"Sit down," he told her.

She hesitated.

"I don't care how angry Reed gets. This is my house, and you're welcome here."

Her knees wobbled. "But…" She gazed into Seth's face. "I don't understand."

His voice went soft, his expression turning patient. "And neither do I. And that's why you're going to explain it to me."

Niki had no idea what to say. "You're not angry?"

"I don't know. I don't yet know what you did." He gestured to the sofa behind her. "Why don't you sit down and tell me?"

Her glance went reflexively to the archway where Reed and then Katrina had disappeared.

"Don't worry about them," said Seth.

"I'm very worried about them."

It didn't matter how much more she explained to Seth. The damage was done. Reed wasn't going to get over this. He was never going to forgive her for lying.

"Sit," Seth told her gently.

She did so.

Seth took the other end of the sofa.

She waited for a question, but he seemed to be waiting for an answer.

She cracked first. "My name is Niki Gerard," she began a little shakily. "My mother was Gabriella Gerard. She did just die, and I found out about Wilton and Reed and Caleb from her papers, exactly as I said. But it was in D.C., not Boston. And I came here." A soft sob escaped from her throat, and it took her a minute to recover. "I came here because I was afraid to stay in D.C."

The words began to pour out of Niki, her mother's affairs, the danger of the secrets the men had apparently revealed, judges, politicians, millionaires. She told him about the missing diary and her growing fear for her own safety.

"When I first met Reed and Caleb," she said, "they were strangers. I knew people were after me, people with the resources to comb the world if they wanted. I didn't dare use my passport, my driver's license, my credit cards. I couldn't board a plane or rent a car or get a hotel room. I couldn't tell anyone, *anyone,* who I was."

Her throat was aching, and her voice fell away.

"Why now?" asked Seth.

"Why now?" came a second voice overtop.

Niki glanced up to find Katrina standing in the archway.

"Why tell us now?" she repeated.

"I felt guilty," said Niki. "I've felt guilty for a very long time. But when the truck washed away tonight, and I thought I might die, I knew you had to know. You have the right to know what I've done, who I am."

"Who's after you?" came Reed's deep voice, and he emerged from the shadows.

He still looked angry, every six-feet-four, muscle-bound inch of him.

Niki had to force herself to speak. "I don't know. I couldn't find the diary and my mother didn't speak about her private matters. I don't know even know what the secrets were. If I could find the diary, at least I could narrow it down."

"You've searched your mother's house? All the obvious places?" asked Seth.

Niki nodded.

"Could someone have stolen it?"

"I don't know," Niki answered Seth. "Gabriella was very clever, and she was very careful. I can't imagine she would have made that easy for anyone."

"Why aren't you looking for it?" asked Reed.

"I was. I did. I looked every place I could think of. But then I started to get paranoid. I imagined people were following me."

She gave a pained laugh. With time and distance, she had to wonder if it had been only her imagination.

Katrina moved forward. "You did the right thing."

"She lied to all of us," Reed put in.

Katrina turned sharply to her husband. "To protect herself. Reed, if I didn't know you so well, I'd be afraid of you myself. You can't have expected her to bare her soul the minute she found you."

"Baring her soul and being honest are two different things."

"She's your sister, Reed."

Reed gave a derisive snort.

"It's your responsibility to protect her."

"If you won't," Seth put in staunchly, "I certainly will."

Niki's chest caved in with an ache, and a tear escaped from her eye. She barely knew Seth, and he was standing up for her.

"As far as I'm concerned—" Seth gazed at her "—she's my sister-in-law. And I know Travis will see it the same way. You kick her to the curb, and we'll—"

"Who's kicking anyone to the curb?" Reed shouted.

Niki gasped in a breath that sounded like a sob.

"See what you've done?" Katrina demanded, crossing to Niki and putting an arm around her shoulder.

"What *I've* done? So, I'm the bad guy?"

"Yes, you're the bad guy. You're the one who's yelling."

"I'm not yelling, Katrina." Reed moderated his voice. "I am not yelling. Jeez, can't a guy argue with his younger sister?"

Niki raised a shaky hand to her mouth, tears flowing down her cheeks.

"Oh, man." Reed moved toward her. "Come here, Nellie. I mean Niki."

He folded her into his strong embrace. He'd hugged her before, but something was different this time. His arms held her tight to his broad chest, lifting her right off the ground.

"I love you," he told her gruffly. "Don't be afraid of me. You're my family, and I'll never hurt you."

She managed a nod.

"But don't lie to me anymore."

She shook her head.

"We'll figure this out. Between us and the Jacobs, you've got four brothers now, and you're safe here."

Niki thought her heart would burst. They didn't hate her. They weren't going to kick her out into the storm.

"I love you, too," she whispered to Reed.

"That's the spirit."

"I don't think we should tell anyone," said Katrina.

"Katrina's right," Seth put in. "People are still out there looking for her."

"We need to find the diary," said Reed.

"She's safe for now. That's enough," Seth argued.

"Only for now though," said Reed.

"What do *you* want us to do?" Seth asked Niki.

Niki stepped away from Reed, slowly bringing herself back under control. Her chest was still tight, but it was from happiness and relief instead of dread. "I want to hide here in Lyndon Valley and forget Niki Gerard ever existed."

Katrina smiled and reached out to hold her hand.

Reed spoke up. "You could change your name to Nellie Terrell."

"They keep records of that," said Seth. He considered for a moment. "The best thing to do right now is nothing."

"That doesn't solve anything," said Reed. "It only postpones it."

"I've been postponing it for three months," Niki pointed out. She could do it a while longer.

"You start mentioning Niki Gerard," said Seth. "And all of a sudden Lyndon Valley pops up on somebody's radar."

Reed clenched his jaw in obvious frustration.

"We do nothing," Katrina decreed.

"I'm telling Caleb," said Reed.

"Should I do that?" Niki felt honor bound to volunteer.

Reed smiled. "No," he told her. "I should do that. Caleb's temper is an acquired taste. Trust me, you'll be happier out of range."

Niki's stomach clenched all over again.

"Don't scare her like that," Katrina warned.

"You think she should tell him herself?" Reed challenged.

Katrina's expression faltered. "Okay. You do it." Then she smiled at Niki. "It'll be fine."

Niki tried to convince herself it was true.

Having made up his mind to romance the information out of Niki, and after telling his uncle of the plan in order to keep Charles off his back awhile longer, Sawyer approached Niki. She was sitting with Katrina in the third row of bleachers, cheering for Travis who was halfway through his eight seconds on the back of Terminator Too, rumored to be the rangiest bull at the event. The crowd roared its appreciation as Travis hung on tight, his back arched, legs straight, hat flying to the ground while the bull sprang from the deep dirt, swerving right then switchbacking left.

The horn sounded, and the crowd went wild, whoops and cheers coming up from every quarter.

Niki hugged Katrina, grinning from ear to ear. Her laugh was relaxed, her entire posture completely different than last night. To be fair, they'd been battling against a natural disaster last night. But it still seemed like more than that.

As he approached the pair, he couldn't take his eyes off Niki. Her cheeks were flushed. Her eyes were shining. And her fresh, windblown look made her even more beautiful than when she'd been dressed to the nines.

He reminded himself of his thought processes last night. Romancing her was a perfectly reasonable course of action. Nobody had to get hurt. Men and women dated all the time. They started new relationships. Those relationships ended. People moved on from there. It wasn't the end of the world.

If he played his cards right, he could get the information he needed from Niki, gently break it off and get out of her life forever, maybe tell her he'd decided to move back to Montana. She'd be none the wiser, never knowing who he was or that he'd manipulated her for his own ends.

He'd work hard to make sure that was the outcome.

"Nice ride," he commented to the women, sparing a glance for Travis who'd been plucked off the bull by a cowboy on horseback and lowered to the ground.

Travis punched his fist in the air in celebration, while the rodeo clowns and cowboys corralled Terminator Too.

"I bet he wins," said Katrina excitedly, holding up crossed fingers. "Oh, there's Reed. See you later." She stood and skipped down the bleachers to the ground, rushing toward her husband who had just taken first place in the steer wrestling competition.

Sawyer swung up to the third row, setting himself down next to Niki and propping his boot on the rough, bench seat in front.

"Hey," he offered by way of an easy greeting.

"Eight-point-nine!" cried the announcer. "Travis Jacobs ends the day with a phenomenal eight-point-nine score on the back of Terminator Too."

"Woo hoo!" Travis yelled from the rodeo ring, while the crowd cheered him on.

Niki clapped long and loud.

"How're you doing?" Sawyer asked Niki.

"I'm fine. Good show." But she kept her gaze squarely forward, watching Travis.

Sawyer fought a spurt of jealousy. Travis winning the most macho event of the day wasn't at all helpful to his cause. Now that Sawyer had decided romance was his best avenue, he was going to have to get noticed amongst her crowd of admirers.

"Ever been to a rodeo before?" he asked.

"First one. You?"

"In Montana," he replied, neglecting to mention that he'd only been to three of them. He now saw the error in his plan. He was out of his comfort zone, not in a position to show himself in the best light.

"Do you compete?" she asked.

He shook his head, wishing the admission didn't make him feel inadequate. It was a new experience, feeling as though he wasn't accomplished enough to get the girl.

"Too busy fighting in the navy, I guess."

When he saw the expression on her face, he could have kicked himself. His words had sounded defensive. So, he didn't ride bucking bulls? Who cared? There were other measures of success in life and, by any benchmark, he'd achieved quite a few of them.

Travis suddenly appeared, stepping up on the fence in front of them.

"Hey, pretty lady," he called to Niki.

He took two more rails, then vaulted over the top, landing on the dirt in front of her.

"Well done," she called, rising from her seat to hop down to meet him.

He pulled her into a hug, and swung her around. It was all Sawyer could do not to yank her out of his arms.

She gave him a kiss on the cheek.

Thank goodness it wasn't on the mouth.

"How much did you win?" she asked.

"Two-thousand. You want to help me spend it?"

"Katrina told me you were using the money to buy new boots."

"It's a tradition," he admitted. "Catch you later?"

"You bet."

With a final grin for Niki and a wave to Sawyer, Travis walked off.

It belatedly occurred to Sawyer that he should have offered his congratulations to Travis. But he'd been too busy controlling his jealousy. He doubted he could have shaken the man's hand while Travis was holding Niki.

He moved to her side. "Tradition?"

She gave a pretty shrug. "Apparently, rodeo winnings are spent on custom-designed boots."

"Ought to be some pretty nice boots," Sawyer mused.

Niki stuck out a running shoe. "I could get into two-thousand-dollar boots."

"Yeah?" His mind went off on a dangerous tangent, picturing something high and leather, with a spike heel and a mini skirt.

She put a hand on his arm to balance herself. "A little something from Saks."

He'd buy the woman anything she wanted, from Saks Fifth Avenue or anywhere else on the planet.

"You want to grab something to eat?" he asked gruffly.

"Don't you have to head back to your ranch?"

"Not right away. I was planning to have dinner first."

Her hand left his arm, and she craned her neck, looking around the grounds. "I wonder what Katrina and Reed are planning to do."

"I can drive you back to the Valley," said Sawyer. "Just give them a call and let them know you're with me."

There was no way he wanted to turn this into a foursome. Or worse, add Travis the champion bull rider to the mix. Dylan would understand if Sawyer left alone with Niki in their loaner truck. His ranch manager would find his own way home.

"I've heard great things about the Riverfront Grill," he added.

She was still glancing around. "Probably everybody will—"

"Nellie."

She turned.

"You and me. Dinner. What do you say?"

She looked confused. "You mean…"

He couldn't seem to stop a grin at her confusion. "Are you usually this daft?"

"No. I mean. Not usually. I didn't think…"

"Well, start thinking."

She cocked her head ever so slightly. "Is this a date?"

"Give the girl a gold star." He found himself easing in a little closer. "It's the least I can do."

Her teeth scraped over her lower lip, and her cheeks flushed. "After last night?"

"After I nearly drowned you," he put in quickly.

Until she blushed, he hadn't been thinking about their kisses. But now that was all he could think about.

"We've already had our first kiss," he offered, surprised by her apparent unease. "And our second. So, that's out of the way."

She was a sophisticated, worldly woman. She must have dated dozens of guys a whole lot more intimidating than a Montana cowboy. Then again, maybe the problem was that she didn't like cowboys. Maybe this whole blending in with the locals thing was going to backfire on him.

"I clean up good," he offered.

"I saw that last night."

"I can do it again. You won't be stuck across the table from a smelly cowboy."

"That's not what worries me."

"Then tell me what worries you."

"You don't smell," she put in.

"Glad to hear it. So, what worries you, Nellie?" He couldn't help but hope she'd own up to something, any little thing from her past that would give him a toehold into an advantageous conversation.

The silence between them stretched, while the announcer

prattled on, and the crowd whooped and clapped at the award-
ing of the prize purses.

"Nothing," Niki finally answered. "Okay, Sawyer. I'll go
on a date with you."

Seven

Walking toward the river, across the trimmed lawn after dinner at the Riverfront Grill, Niki realized she hadn't felt this relaxed in months, maybe not in years. Her brother Reed knew the truth, and he'd forgiven her. What's more, he'd offered to help her in any way he could.

He'd called Caleb last night, and had then sworn to Niki that Caleb had taken the news well. He wasn't upset. He understood why she'd made the decision to keep her secret. Of course, the call had taken an hour. She could only speculate that Reed had done some serious talking to bring their brother around.

"We can go have dessert on the deck," Sawyer offered, walking beside her on the cobblestone path.

"I want to see the waterfall," Niki responded. "Before it gets dark."

The sun was hanging low near the western mountain peaks. It had turned the wispy clouds to pink, and the sky was going purple above them.

"The waitress said it was half a mile."

"What's the matter, Sawyer? You out of shape?"

His chuckle was low and warm, strumming through her. "I don't want you tripping in the dark."

"Don't worry about me." She wasn't worried.

For the first time in, oh, such a long time, she wasn't worried. Her future might be uncertain, but she wasn't alone. And she could stay in Lyndon Valley. She could stay here just as long as she liked.

She found herself breaking into a trot.

"Race you," she called over her shoulder, heading for the packed dirt path that ran along the river. The hill fell steeply down to the water beside it, but there was a low guardrail along the edge.

Sawyer caught up almost instantly, positioning himself on the outside of the pathway, between Niki and the hillside.

"Afraid I'll fall over?" she teased as she ran.

"I'd hate to lose you on the first date."

"Does that mean there'll be a second?"

Yesterday, she would have said dating Sawyer was a ridiculous dream. But everything had changed. Not that she could tell him her true identity. The family was keeping it a closely held secret. But it did mean she could continue to be Nellie Cooper. And Nellie Cooper could have a crush on her sexy, new neighbor. Especially if that sexy, new neighbor seemed to like her back.

"I hope so," Sawyer told her.

He took her hand, bringing her knuckles to his lips to kiss her as they jogged.

Their gazes met, and she stumbled.

He swiftly grabbed her, swirling her to a halt, pulling her safely against his body, chuckling at her clumsiness.

"That was your fault," she pointed out.

"I'll take the blame every time," he agreed easily. "If this is how it ends up." He smoothly turned to face her, keeping his arms wrapped loosely around her waist. He brushed her hair back from her cheek.

The atmosphere shifted between them, awareness sizzling in the dusky light. He was an incredibly sexy man, handsome, strong, intelligent and confident.

"I want to kiss you, Nellie Cooper."

She was taken aback by his gallant manner. "Are you asking permission?"

"I am."

She searched his expression. "Who are you, and what have you done with Sawyer Smith?"

He smiled. "I'm very sorry about last night."

She wasn't. What woman didn't like to dress up, go out on the town and be swept off her feet by a sexy cowboy?

"I don't know what came over me," he said.

"I kind of hoped it was me."

He tugged her closer. "You're not saying yes, Nellie."

She gave a tiny, noble bow, fighting a grin as she stared into his eyes.

He stared right back, irises darkening to indigo. His fingertips twitched against her waist, but he didn't make a move.

"Are you going to stand there and let me tease you?" she challenged.

"I'm waiting for you to say yes."

"And if I don't?"

"I'll assume you mean no."

"Seriously?"

"Seriously." He waited.

Longing came to life within her, sending a zigzag of awareness to her limbs. Her gaze moved to his mouth, remembering the touch of his full lips, their sweet taste, their firm texture. The way they gave and took at the same time.

She knew she should break down and tell him yes, but there was something electrifying about their standoff.

She walked her fingers playfully up his chest. "You didn't wait for a yes last night."

He trapped her hand. "That was a mistake."

"I thought it was sexy."

He jerked her flush against him, and there was an edge to his tone. "Every single thing about you is sexy."

"Have I gone too far?"

"Depends on what you're trying to do."

"Make you kiss me."

He sucked in a breath. "Okay, *that's* a yes."

"You're cheat—"

His mouth swooped down on hers.

She remembered this—his incredible kiss, the feel of his strong arms around her. Last night, she'd been guarded, reluctantly swept along by passion. But today, she stepped into it. Her world didn't seem quite so precarious, Sawyer quite so forbidden.

She opened to him, stretching up, meeting his tongue, while her own arms wound around his neck, steadying her on the uneven walkway. Their bodies flush to one another, he shifted, one leg slightly between hers. His hand cupped the back of her head, deepening the kiss.

Then, suddenly, he gasped, pulling back, touching his forehead to hers, sucking in deep breaths. Niki was breathless herself. But she missed his kiss, and tipped her head, tilting in an invitation.

"We're in full view of the restaurant," he reminded her.

She swore under her breath.

"Agreed," he offered. Then he captured her hand, entwining their fingers as he put a little distance between them. "Let's go see the falls."

Niki had to remind her feet to move. She clumsily fell into step beside him. But it took her heart a few seconds to calm down, brain a bit longer to find equilibrium. The roar of the falls grew in the distance, while the path followed the curve of the river.

"Another average kiss?" she couldn't stop herself from asking.

"What?" He seemed to shake himself out of a daze.

"You told me my kisses were average."

He frowned. "When did I do that?"

"In the river. After you rescued me."

He seemed to consider that for a moment. "I told you *my* kisses were average."

She waited, wondering if he'd turn it into a compliment. He didn't.

"Sawyer?"

"Yeah?" His tone was a bit gruff, but she was feeling too carefree to let it upset her.

"Your kisses aren't average."

His hand squeezed down on hers. "Here are the falls." He pointed to a wall of white, foaming water.

"They're huge," Niki whistled, quickening her pace.

"One of the longest vertical drops in the state, so they say," Sawyer remarked.

A few clusters of people were standing beside the chain-link fence that lined the cliff's edge. Behind them were benches and a few gazebos dotting the lawn.

"The sign says they light them at night," he told her.

Niki glanced at the setting sun. "Can we wait to see?"

"Of course."

They paused beside the fence. He let go of her hand to place his around her shoulders. The spray dampened her face, her hair, the front of her shirt. The sound of the water was deafening where it crashed at the bottom of the cliff, roiling into streams of white foam that cascaded down the riverbed, over boulders, cutting into the side of the channel. It was somehow mesmerizing.

"Can you imagine riding down that?" Niki found herself venturing.

"The fall would probably kill you."

"Well, I wouldn't jump from here."

"I wouldn't jump from anywhere."

She shifted to look at him. "Have you ever done white-water rafting?"

He met her gaze, and she couldn't help but drink in and appreciate his tousled, windblown looks.

"I have," he responded. "Kayaking, too, and I've also taken on very big waves on the ocean."

"Was it fun?"

"It was exhilarating."

"Is that fun?"

"It was fun for me."

"But it's dangerous, right?" Her gaze went back to the rushing rapids. She couldn't help but imagine bobbing over them in a raft.

"Depends," he drawled.

"On?"

"On whether or not you take a former naval officer along for protection."

Niki grinned, casting him a sidelong gaze. "If I was to take a former naval officer along for protection?"

His hand moved around to the curve of her waist. "Then, you'd be perfectly safe."

"Good to know." She tried to gauge and quantify her fear after the flood and after getting towed away by the river current at the water-polo game. She and water seemed to be having a power struggle.

"Nellie?"

"Yes?"

"You want to try white-water rafting?"

"I think I do." Her heart beat a little faster at the thought of shooting a river, but she didn't want to let that stop her. She was in the mood to confront her fears, take control of her life, and this seemed like a good place to start.

"You can just come right out and ask, you know." There was a knowing chuckle in his voice.

"What do you mean?"

"I mean—" he brushed the tip of her nose with his index finger "—you don't have to manipulate a man into doing what you want."

Something stilled inside Niki. Her fear was replaced by annoyance. She didn't manipulate men, that was Gabriella's weakness. "I don't do that."

He did a double take of her expression. "Okay."

She eased slightly away from him. "I mean it, Sawyer. I don't manipulate men."

"I said okay."

"That's not an admirable character trait."

"I'm sorry."

"I don't want you to apologize."

"Then, what do you want?"

What she wanted, was to not be her mother. Gabriella was the master of mind games with men. She got what she wanted, and they didn't know what hit them. Winning had never made her particularly happy, but she seemed compelled to do it with every man she came across.

Niki also didn't want to be the person she'd been for the past three months.

"Nellie?" Sawyer prompted. "What do you want?"

"I want not to be afraid."

"Of white-water rafting?"

"Yes." It wasn't her only fear, not even her biggest fear. But she'd told her brothers the truth, and she was ready to move on to something else. Maybe she'd work her way up to confronting her mother's lovers.

"Then that's what we'll do," he told her, snagging her at the waist and pulling her close once again. He kissed her damp hair. "We'll take a thrilling, exhilarating trip down some white-water rapids. I guarantee you'll love it. And, afterward, you won't be afraid anymore."

"I won't," she vowed.

"Look," he told her, nodding to the waterfall. "The lights are coming on."

A rainbow of lights came on beneath the water, layering their way down the falls, pink to purple, to blue and green, with white pot lights glimmering beneath the foliage that clung to the rocks. The water danced, and mist rose up, making the atmosphere a cloud of pastel magic.

"Gorgeous," Niki breathed.

"Stunning," Sawyer agreed.

When she glanced up to smile at him, he was gazing at her, not the waterfall.

"Thanks for bringing me here," she whispered.

"I'll take you anywhere you want to go," he vowed.

Sawyer could have seduced Niki last night. Or he could have let her seduce him. Either would have had a fantastic outcome.

But he'd ruthlessly held back, dropping her off at the Terrell ranch, safe in the bosom of her family, with little more than a fleeting good-night kiss.

While no one would accuse any Layton of misguided chivalry, Sawyer wasn't morally bankrupt, either. At least, not yet. Though making love with Niki could well put him over the edge.

Plus, he was starting to truly like her. Maybe it was because his expectations had been so low in the beginning, but he'd been pleasantly surprised. She was bright and funny, and he hadn't seen any of the conniving nerve he'd imagined from seeing her pictures and hearing stories of her mother.

He was now completely certain she didn't know who he was. And he wasn't even sure anymore that she was plotting against his uncle, or against anyone else for that matter.

He had to consider the possibility that she was simply trying to keep herself safe in the middle of a senseless situation. If that was true, she had a very big problem. Sawyer might be the first to find her, but he wouldn't be the last, and not everyone would take this low-key approach to getting information.

At the breakfast table with Dylan, Sawyer's cell phone chimed.

"She was heading back to Denver today," Dylan was saying. He'd been describing his evening with the brunette he'd met at the rodeo dance.

"That's a good thing?" Sawyer asked as he extracted his phone.

"Good thing for me," said Dylan. "She was fun and all, but I don't see happily ever after in the cards for us."

"You never see happily ever after in the cards," Sawyer replied, noting his uncle Charles' office number on the screen.

"That's because I stack the deck," said Dylan.

Sawyer didn't have any argument with that logic. He raised the phone to his ear. "Charles," he greeted while Dylan gave him an eye-roll.

"I need a status report," his uncle came straight to the point.

"You know the status," said Sawyer. "I found her, and I'm trying to figure out where she's hidden the diary."

"You said you were going to seduce her. What's taking so long?"

"I said romance, not seduce." Sawyer regretted having told him anything at all.

"Don't play with semantics. Get it done. The midterm elections are right around the corner."

"I've got another date with her. Besides, we've got a few months to play with," Sawyer replied.

"You do *not* have a few months. I want this settled and resolved asap."

"I'm working my way in," said Sawyer.

"Do you need more manpower?"

"It's a one-man job."

Dylan coughed out a laugh, and Sawyer sent him a glare.

"And are you the man for it?" Charles demanded.

"Yes," Sawyer responded with conviction.

"Then get on with it."

"Uncle, you are going to have to acquire some patience."

"Easy for you to say. It's not your career that's on the line."

"I'm also not the one who screwed around on his wife."

Dylan's brow rose in obvious surprise and clear admiration.

"Don't get cocky with me, young man," Charles sputtered. "I still control this family, and that includes the money."

"Yeah?" For some reason, Sawyer felt more than the usual impatience with his uncle's arrogance. "Well, I'm perfectly employable in the US Navy."

"Is that a threat?" asked Charles.

"It's a statement of fact."

"Go ahead. I'd like to see you *try* to live on a Lieutenant's salary."

Sawyer regretted letting the conversation get off track. "You have to leave this to me, Charles. I'm the man on the ground, and I'm doing what's best."

"Do it faster."

"I'll call you as soon as I know something. Goodbye." He hit the disconnect button before Charles could say anything else.

Dylan was the first to speak. "You decided to poke the bear?"

"What's he going to do?" Sawyer tucked the phone away. "He knows damn well I'm his best chance to solve this problem."

"Don't get me wrong. I think your family should have ganged up on the bastard years ago. I just wonder why now."

"Because this isn't going to work his way."

"Nothing ever works his way. But you usually humor him."

"Guess I'm in a bad mood." Sawyer polished off his coffee.

"Sexually frustrated, perhaps?"

Sawyer didn't dignify the accusation with an answer. Although it was completely true.

"I'm taking her white-water rafting," he noted.

Dylan asked in a wry voice, "Did you read somewhere that that was romantic?"

Sawyer frowned at Dylan.

"Did you even consider dinner and a movie?"

"She wants to go white-water rafting," Sawyer countered. "Just because you're completely unimaginative about your dates…"

"I got lucky after the dance. That's not unimaginative."

Sawyer grunted a noncommittal response.

But Dylan didn't let it go. "I'm just sayin' if you want to compare techniques."

"*You're* the one who told me to romance her, not seduce her."

Dylan smirked into his coffee cup. "Doesn't mean I can't enjoy your pain."

Sawyer pushed away from the table. "I've got work to do."

He'd found a white-water rafting outfit a couple of hours away, and now he needed to track down Niki and invite her along.

He rose. Just thinking about her made his steps a little lighter. His frustration over his uncle's stubbornness evaporated, and his mood improved.

"Don't wait up," he told Dylan as he crossed for the door, snagging his cowboy hat.

"Big talker," Dylan jeered.

Sawyer turned and gave a cocky grin.

A flash of worry crossed Dylan's face. "Don't do it. I'm just messin' with you here. Don't screw it all up by sleeping with her."

"Have a little faith," Sawyer returned.

"I have too much faith. I've seen you in action."

"Nice of you to finally admit it." Sawyer swung the door closed behind him.

He stuffed his hat on his head, chose the closest pickup truck, and peeled out of the yard, bouncing down the driveway toward the Terrell place.

Niki had expected a solid raft, a wide, stable craft with eight passengers and an experienced guide at the tiller. Instead, she was standing on the River Adventures dock, next to what looked like an inflatable kayak, narrow, wobbly, with only two seats, and not a guide in sight.

"It'll be fine," Sawyer reassured her, checking the clips and cinching down the straps on her bright orange life jacket. "You'll have a blast."

"What if I panic?" She struggled to hold on to her courage.

First the white water, she had told herself. Then she'd figure out how to deal with the bad guys.

"What if we tip over?" she found herself asking.

"Then I'll rescue you." He handed her a two-ended paddle. "I've done it before."

"Be serious," she pressed.

"That's what the life jacket's for. It'll keep you afloat until I get to you. Besides, the rapids are only grade four. We probably won't go over."

"Probably?" Her voice had gone embarrassingly high.

"Nellie."

"What?"

"This is going to be fun."

She stared at him, trying to ascertain the level of confidence on his face. He looked plenty confident. He also looked relaxed. He looked like he was laughing at her.

"You've done this before?" she confirmed, telling herself to buck up.

"Many, many times. In smaller boats and in bigger boats."

"But, not this size."

His face broke into a grin. "Has anybody ever told you, you worry too much?"

"Many, many times," she muttered, thinking of her mother.

Gabriella had called Niki a worrywart. It was true that most of her worry had proved pointless. They'd usually gotten away with Gabriella's schemes.

"You don't need to worry."

"That's what my mother used to say."

"And was she right?"

"Don't worry, Niki," Niki parroted. "The sign on the back-stage door doesn't mean *us* when it says No Admittance. Niki, you don't *have* to be on the guest list if you know what to say. Niki, speed signs are for people who *don't* know how to flirt with police officers."

Sawyer grinned. "I think I might have liked your mother."

"Everybody liked my mother," said Niki. "That's how she got away with it."

He moved to where the small craft was tied up, crouching to release the ropes. "For today," he said to Niki. "You truly don't need to worry. I promise I won't speed down the river."

"That's a comfort," said Niki, squaring her shoulders.

"You get in the front," said Sawyer. "And I'll launch us. Remember, paddle when I tell you, like I showed you. If we do go into the water—"

Niki shot him a warning look over the bulky life jacket.

"If we do go into the water," he repeated. "Keep your feet downstream. Try to avoid the white water, because there are rocks underneath it, and angle toward the shore."

"I'm too young to die," she told him.

"This was your idea," he reminded her.

"I thought it would be different."

"How?"

"I thought we'd have a professional guide."

"I am a professional guide."

"You know what I mean."

His tone was patient. "Nellie, recreational river guides can be certified in a few weeks. It takes years to get my level of naval training. I'm better than a guide."

Her confidence level inched up. "Yeah?"

"Yeah. Now, get in the boat."

Niki drew a bracing breath. "All right."

It was now or never. She maneuvered carefully into the boat, balancing one hand on the dock as she compensated for the stiff life jacket. Beneath the jacket, she wore her bathing suit, covered by a little, cotton sundress, all topped with a white baseball cap.

The rental company provided a lunch, a blanket, rain jackets, and a first-aid kit, all packed in watertight containers and strapped to the inside of the tandem raft. She settled into the molded plastic seat.

"Here we go," Sawyer called from behind, and the raft moved out into the river.

It swayed slightly, first to one side then the other as he settled into his own seat. The movement only ramped up the butterflies in her stomach.

"Paddle on both sides," he called.

Niki dug in, moving the paddle through the water on her right, then on her left. Right, left, right, left.

As they neared the center of the river, Sawyer pointed them downstream. They bobbed along, and the paddling was easy. The little raft pitched and rolled as it gained speed in the swift, smooth current. The mountain scenery moved past, leaves rustling in the trees, birds flitting from branch to branch, and a few fluffy clouds high above in the blue sky.

"You're doing great," Sawyer called from behind.

"This is fun," she returned, paddling in rhythm.

They rounded the first bend in the river, and the building and dock owned by the rental company disappeared behind them. The river was, maybe, thirty feet wide, snaking its way through quiet wilderness.

White water appeared in the distance, rock faces rising up on either side, with one huge boulder sticking up in the middle.

"I'm taking us through the left channel," Sawyer advised. "It'll get bumpy, but don't worry. It's plenty deep, and we won't hit anything below."

The raft sped up, and Niki gripped her paddle, nerves rising again. They went up a roller, then steeply down the other side, missing the boulder by a few feet. She forgot to paddle as they leaped sharply up again, sweeping in a turn, bouncing over rapids that splashed her from head to toe.

She gasped at the cold, and she could hear Sawyer's laughter behind her.

"Well done," he called encouragingly.

"I didn't do anything." She hadn't paddled a stroke.

"Doesn't matter," he told her easily. "I can maneuver it by myself."

The water smoothed out again, the raft bobbing gently up and down as they whispered along. Niki resumed paddling. The sun was warm on her head, the wind from their movement fresh across her wet face. A pair of mallards swam in the shallows of a back eddy, taking flight as the raft moved past. A fish jumped, clearing the water, its silvery body flashing in the sun.

The sound of the river grew louder.

"You'll want to hang on tight through this," said Sawyer.

She twisted around to look at him. "Is something about to happen?"

"There's a small waterfall around the bend."

"Are you joking?"

"It's little. More a series of rapids than anything. But there'll be a drop at the end. Hang on tight like I said, and let me do the work."

The sound of the water grew louder. She glimpsed a plume of white spray shooting up in the distance, reminding her of the massive falls from last night. She blocked that image from her mind. Sawyer had said the waterfall was little.

It looked little.

Okay, maybe it looked medium.

There were an awful lot of rocks sticking up in the rapids.

The raft moved swiftly forward, and she gripped tight as they bounced their way down the incline of rapids. Sawyer took them around the rocks and through the deepest points that looked dark and mysterious. Although Niki's stomach lurched a few times, she couldn't help a grin that grew on her face.

This really was exhilarating.

She braced herself for the little falls, gripping tight to the handles and her paddle. The raft launched over the edge, dropping into a pool below, and a wave of water soaked her to the skin. The boat spun in a complete circle in the small whirlpool before Sawyer got them out the other side.

She sputtered and laughed, as Sawyer pointed them downriver again.

"That was a blast," she sang out. "Are there more?"

"There are more," he answered her.

She dipped her paddle in and began to help again. Her nerves had settled down. She felt proud of herself. She was conquering another fear.

"Where have you done this before?" she asked.

"Washington State, California, Alaska."

"You've been to Alaska?"

"The navy likes to drop by Anchorage every once in a while."

"Never been there." Niki paddled harder. "My mother wasn't the Alaska type."

"What type was she?"

"Bright lights, big city."

"Like Vegas?"

"Like Manhattan, LA, Paris. She enjoyed shopping on Rodeo Drive and dining at Boa's."

"Did she ever get married?"

Niki couldn't help but smile at that. "Never. She used to tell me that the best way to get a man to stop paying attention to you was to marry him."

Sawyer was silent for a long while. "Are *you* that cynical, Nellie?"

"I'm nothing like my mother."

"How so?"

Niki tried to put her feelings into words. "I'm not fond of drama, and I don't need to be the center of the universe."

"The two of you didn't get along?" he asked.

"Quite the contrary. We got along great. She adored her baby girl. And for sheer, outright fun, you could not beat Gab—my mother. She took me shopping, to amusement parks, to parties and plays, and the circus. When I was little, I had a pink, SugarDoll bedroom, with a canopied bed, purple carpet and unicorns painted on the ceiling. It was the other people in her life that took the brunt of it."

"What was the brunt of it?"

"To adore her, to worship her and to believe with all your heart it was mutual."

"But, it wasn't?"

"It wasn't. And I liked some of them. They were very nice, perfectly nice, classy and kind."

"I take it we're talking about her boyfriends."

"They were lovers more than boyfriends," said Niki. Though she hadn't understood it at the time. "I suspect most of them, maybe all of them, were married. My mother liked having the power in the relationship."

"Did she blackmail them?"

Niki stopped abruptly to peer at him. "What makes you ask that?"

Gabriella might have been crafty, but she wasn't a criminal.

"You said she liked power."

"Not that kind of power. How did *you* get so cynical?"

"You're going to want to hang on again."

As soon as he said it, Niki heard the roar of the rapids. She turned to see a patch of foaming water.

"Should I paddle?" she called.

"Just hang on tight!"

Eight

Despite her initial nervousness, it was obvious Niki had had a great time on the river. Sawyer was impressed with her endurance for paddling, and she quickly became fearless going over the rapids and down the small falls. They stopped for lunch, then they stopped at a number of picturesque beaches along the way. They even portaged back up one beach to shoot a waterfall for a second time.

When they eventually reached the pullout point at the Sky-high Inn, they were exhausted, and the sun was sinking behind the Rockies. Attendants at the five-star hotel helped them pull the tandem raft onto the wharf. As Sawyer had arranged, there was an employee from the raft rental outfit on hand to return the boat and give Sawyer the keys to his truck, which was now parked in the hotel parking lot.

His flexible water shoes squished against the boards of the dock as they made their way toward the resort. He caught Niki looking longingly toward an outdoor restaurant. It was full of smartly dressed waiters and white tablecloths that billowed in the light breeze.

Sawyer was starving, too.

"Anywhere we can grab a bite to eat?" he asked the wharf attendant who was close behind them.

The young man glanced at his watch. "You can get hot dogs and hamburgers by the pool. But the poolside concession closes in about fifteen minutes."

Sawyer glanced down at Niki. She looked about as excited by a hot dog as he felt.

"Yeah, that's not going to do it," he muttered under his breath.

He captured her hand, angling them toward the main staircase.

"What?" she asked, taking in the well-dressed guests, the uniformed porters and the elegant, airy, polished-beam lobby visible through a massive wall of glass.

"Are you hungry?" he asked.

"I don't think we should go in there."

"They have a nice restaurant."

"We're dripping wet."

"We'll dry."

A doorman opened a glass door in front of them, giving a polite nod of greeting. "Good evening, sir. Welcome to the Skyhigh Inn."

"Good evening," Sawyer returned as they passed through the doorway. "See?" he said to Niki. "No problem."

"I'm a little self-conscious." She attempted to rub some of the wrinkles out of her mottled purple sundress. "I'm leaving tracks on the marble floor."

"Careful you don't slip," he advised.

"Everyone is staring."

It was true. The guests were not nearly so well-trained as the doorman. Finely dressed ladies looked aghast, while *gentlemen*—Sawyer used the term loosely—stared unabashedly at the way Niki's little dress was plastered to her body.

They made it to the front desk, and a friendly woman greeted them. "Welcome to the Skyhigh Inn."

"We'd like a room to clean up," Sawyer told her. "And then reservations at the restaurant. Out on the patio, if that's possible."

She punched a few keys in her computer. "We're very busy tonight," she cautioned. "All I'm showing as available is a vista suite on the VIP floor."

"We'll take it," said Sawyer, dropping his credit card on the counter. "And dinner?"

She took in their appearance. "There is a dress code in the restaurant."

"I'm sure you have some kind of clothing shop in the hotel?"

"Yes, sir. We do. Mario's through the main hallway, and Giselle's Boutique right next door."

"Can you send a few options up to the suite? Something that will meet the restaurant dress code?"

"Of course." She gave Niki a sweeping glance, obviously assessing her likely dress size. Then she did the same with Sawyer. "I'll have them sent right up."

"Thank you." Sawyer tucked his credit card back in his pocket.

"Your key," said the woman. "Number eight-o-two. Take the elevators behind the fountain. You'll need to insert your key card to access the eighth floor. I'll let the maitre d' know to expect you."

"Thank you," Sawyer said again. Then he took Niki's hand.

People still stared as they made their way to the elevator. But they were quickly inside one of the cars, and the doors closed behind them.

He pressed the button for the eighth floor.

Niki was watching him curiously.

"What?" he asked her.

"You're reminding me of my mother."

"I'm not conning our way past security. We have every right to be here."

"Not that. I'm talking about extravagance and expediency.

You see no reason why the world shouldn't revolve around you."

Truth was, he didn't. The hotel was here to serve guests, and he was a guest. Wet or dry, his money was as good as the next person's.

"Is that a bad thing?"

"No. But I'd never have crossed the lobby alone looking like a river rat."

"We're river rats with a high credit limit."

She was studying him in a way that made him nervous. "There's something about you."

"You mean other than my being a river rat?"

"I've been hanging around cowboys for a while now, and you make me feel like I'm back in, uh, Boston."

"Are you telling me I have more class than your average cowboy?"

"Maybe." But she was still studying him.

Sawyer could have kicked himself for the mistake. He was swaggering around the place like some kind of wealthy businessman, paying for thousand-dollar-a-night hotel suites on a whim. He realized he was trying to impress her, and that was foolish. He wasn't here to impress her. He was here to con her.

"Bullheadedness is a cowboy trait," he put in.

"I suppose," she allowed.

Just then the elevator doors slid open, revealing the opulent hallway of the VIP floor. He wondered if he should pretend to be in awe. But he supposed it was a little too late for that.

They found their suite, opening double doors to a large, brightly decorated living room, a dining area, a substantial bedroom and bath, and a deck that overlooked the river.

While Niki showered, a butler dropped off three potential outfits for each of them. Then, when Sawyer stepped out of the bathroom, freshly shampooed and shaved, he found Niki had chosen a black and burgundy cocktail dress. She was scrutinizing her appearance in front of a full-length mirror, and he immediately stopped caring that he'd gone out of character to get them here.

Her lithe body was hugged by a black sheath with horizontal slashes of burgundy. The hem was at midthigh. Her shoulders were bare, the dress held up by a distinctive, sequined, halted collar that mimicked a necklace.

"What do you think?"

He couldn't seem to keep the huskiness out of his tone. "You clean up good, Nellie Cooper."

"I don't have any shoes."

"In the truck?" he asked.

He'd already had a porter bring up his cowboy boots. He figured they'd be fine with his slacks and jacket. This was Colorado, after all.

"The only thing I have in the truck is a pair of bright red runners," she told him. Then she glanced at her bare feet, as if picturing the shoes. "But, maybe..."

He laughed, picking up the phone. "What size?"

The hotel boutique found a pair of rhinestone flats in her size, tiny and delicate. Wearing them, it looked like Niki had sparkling, bare feet. For some reason, they were the sexiest things Sawyer had ever seen.

He watched them flash under the lights as they crossed the lobby to the restaurant. When the maitre d' seated them next to the rail on the deck, and her feet disappeared beneath the white table cloth, Sawyer fought his disappointment.

"You enjoyed rafting?" he asked.

It was fully dark now, and the stars were bright in the black sky overhead. A small candle flickered in a glass holder between them.

"It was fantastic," she replied, green eyes shining. "I've never taken adventure vacations. But I'm starting to wonder if I should consider them."

"You should," Sawyer responded, both surprised and impressed by her enthusiasm.

"Maybe mountain climbing. Maybe skydiving."

"Have we created a monster?" he asked.

"I'm embarking on a little self-improvement."

"Through adventure sports."

"By facing my fears. You know, you confront them, and they lose their power."

"Often true," he agreed. "But, do me a favor. Get some lessons before you conquer skydiving."

"That's a very good idea. I'm sure there are many people out there who could teach me."

I could teach you.

Sawyer confessed to himself that he'd love to teach her river rafting, mountain climbing, skydiving, or anything else. He also confesssed that line of thought was entirely unrealistic, but he determinedly swept the worry aside. Just for dinner, just for the evening, he was going to forget about everything but Niki's company.

"There are definitely people who could teach you," he affirmed.

"Then that's what I'll do," she said with conviction. "Maybe hang gliding."

"Look out, world."

She grinned, and he couldn't stop himself from reaching for her hand. It was warm, soft under his fingers, but he knew it was also strong. She was strong. She was completely unexpected.

"Any blisters from paddling?" he asked.

Her hand flipped palm up. "Right here." She pointed to the base of her middle fingers.

He lifted the hand, leaning forward to kiss the sore spot.

"A cocktail before dinner?" their waiter interrupted.

Sawyer raised a brow at Niki.

"Wine?" she asked.

He watched her expression, making sure she was agreeing with him as he spoke to the waiter. "Something smooth in an old-world cabernet sauvignon. Two-thousand-seven, if you've got it. Oak more than fruit. Maybe Rothchilds. But I'm open to suggestions."

Niki nodded her agreement, a smile growing on her face.

"I'll speak to the Sommelier," said the waiter. "Would you like to consult with him?"

Sawyer shook his head. He didn't want to waste his time talking to some guy about wines. "Go ahead and surprise us."

"Very good, sir. Would you care to order any appetizers to get started?"

Niki perked up. "Something spicy?"

"We have a lovely baked brie with jalapeno chutney."

She gave a nod.

"We'll take it," said Sawyer.

"Thanks," said Niki as the waiter departed.

He gave a shrug. "Hey, eat anything you want. I know I'm pretty hungry after all that paddling."

"And portaging. I'm sorry I couldn't help with that."

"You don't need to help me carry something that light."

"All the same." She flexed an arm, struggling to show some biceps. "If I'm going to climb mountains, I'd better start weight training."

An assistant waiter arrived with a basket of breads, and Niki chose a cheese straw.

"Surely building your brother's house would be a good workout." Sawyer took a cheese straw, too.

"It is," she agreed, snapping the stick in half. "But they give me the easy stuff. Not that I blame them. I was pretty useless when I first showed up. I think they were worried I might hurt someone."

"Did you?"

"Not so far." She took a bite. "So, tell me. What's your favorite adventure sport? What's the most fun?"

Fun wasn't exactly how Sawyer would describe some of his adventures. He'd once rappelled out of a helicopter to rescue a distant cousin from a small-time drug lord on a Caribbean island. "Most of what I do is work, skydiving, water rescue, climbing."

"So, you're an adrenaline junkie."

"I wouldn't say that."

"Well, you didn't become a banker, Sawyer Smith. And apparently ranching wasn't risky enough for you." She pointed at him with her cheese straw. "And it's not the safest job in the world. I've seen those bucking broncos and the stampeding cattle."

"I've gone back to ranching now," he responded.

Then again, he was really back to rescuing his family. So, maybe there was some truth to her words.

"But I'm betting you do jump out of airplanes."

"I do," he admitted.

Her smile was wide and self-satisfied. "You're going to be a very fun neighbor, Sawyer Smith."

Sawyer struggled to squelch his guilt. He told himself she'd get over him. Then he tried to tell himself he'd get over her, too.

Niki had never met anyone quite like Sawyer. He made every man she'd ever met look safe and, well, boring. Heading back to the suite after dinner to pick up their belongings, she couldn't help but be aware of his strength, his capability and sexiness as he strode along beside her.

Other than the small kiss on her blistered palm, he hadn't made any romantic moves over dinner. But it might as well have been an all-out seduction for how she was feeling. She was edgy, alert, aroused. She wanted to cling to him like she had at the waterfall, have him run his hands over her like he had at the dance. She wanted to lose herself in the passion that she knew could rise between them.

He opened the suite door, letting her go in first.

A few steps in, she turned. The door swung shut and the latch clicked into place. She made up her mind to give in to her desire.

"Thank you, Sawyer," she told him, stepping forward, snaking her arms around his neck, closing her eyes and lifting her lips for a kiss.

"Nellie." He placed his hands on her shoulders. It felt like he was pushing her away. And he didn't kiss her.

Her eyes popped open. "Is something wrong?"

"No, nothing's wrong." But his expression was tense, and he didn't move, didn't close the gap between them.

She swiftly catalogued the possible reasons. "I'm asking you to kiss me," she assured him.

"It's not that."

She didn't understand. Or maybe she did. A wash of unease settled into her stomach, embarrassment taking hold of her brain. She dropped her arms, stepping back, glancing away.

"Oh. I'm sorry. I misjudged."

"Nellie, it's not—"

"No, no." She held up her palm. "No need to apologize. I didn't mean to put you in an awkward position."

"This is new," he explained.

"Yeah. Sure." Kissing a woman had to be totally new for him. She couldn't bring herself to look at him.

"We barely know each other."

"Obviously, we don't."

"I don't want to—"

She shot him a sharp glare. "You're making it worse."

He clamped his jaw shut.

"I'll get my clothes."

She turned away and heard him curse behind her.

The next second, his hand was on her arm. He was spinning her around, and his mouth came down on hers, wide-open, instantly carnal.

The kiss went on and on, tension and frustration radiating from his body, his muscles stiff, his fists clenched, his lips firm and demanding.

She reveled in the raw sensuality. She didn't know why he'd held back, and she didn't really care. He'd given in now, and her body welcomed his strength, his purpose, his passion.

But then everything changed. His lips went soft. His kisses turned tender. His body enfolded hers, and his hands stroked her hair, cradling her face. He kissed her sweetly and thoroughly.

Moments later, he swept her up into his arms, cradling her. His sizzling gaze locked with hers as he carried her into the bedroom.

When he set her down, he quickly shrugged out of his jacket. Impatient, she plucked at his tie, loosening the knot, dragging the tail through the loop, pulsing desire heating every fiber of her body.

He flicked the single button at the back of her neck, releasing her collar, releasing the dress, which then clung precariously to the tips of her breasts.

He kissed her neck, his lips hot, his tongue teasing her sensitive skin. He made his way toward her shoulder, while her clumsy fingers fumbled with the buttons on his shirt.

With an exclamation, he tore open the shirt, sending the buttons flying, tossing it in a heap in the corner of the room.

"That was only a few hours old," she told him breathlessly, even as her palms went flat against the heat and strength of his chest. She stroked her way up, over his flat nipples, finding the contours of his pecs and shoulders. She found the ridge of a scar, and then another.

She leaned around to kiss it, flicking her tongue against his skin as he had to hers.

He groaned, and she suckled the spot.

His big hands slid down her back, grasping her buttocks, pulling her against his hardness. She ran her fingers through his short hair, kissed her way across his chest, then managed to release his belt.

His hands moved up her thighs, beneath the short dress, discovering she wasn't wearing any panties beneath. She'd had no spare ones, so she hadn't had a choice.

A rumble rose in his throat, and he kissed her deeply, thoroughly. Then he pulled back a fraction of an inch.

"Just so you know," he told her in a strained voice. "Because at some point it's going to matter. I truly hate myself right now. But I am *so* into you. I can't resist. I can't…"

His words were confusing. She didn't understand what he was trying to say, but then he resumed his kisses, his hands tugging her dress. It fell to pool at her feet, and she stopped thinking altogether.

He stripped off his pants, and they were both naked. They fell together on the bed, stretching out. He wrapped one leg across her body, a hand going to her breast, as he continued the mind-blowing kisses that sent heat cascading along her skin and through to her very bones.

They explored each other's bodies, kissing every inch, letting the passion between them build almost unbearably. He finally rose above her, donned a condom and pushed himself slowly, exquisitely, inexorably inside.

Niki had never felt so complete. Her body accommodated the size of him, all but singing with pleasure at the way they were joined.

She automatically arched her hips, tightened her legs around his waist, stretching to meet him as he set a slow rhythm. She kissed him over and over again. Then she stretched her head back, groaning his name while he kissed her neck, her chest, the tips of her breasts.

His pace increased. And she felt a storm brewing inside her, taking her higher, her muscles incredibly taut. He slid a hand beneath her buttocks, lifting her to him, while his breath ran ragged in her ear.

"Niki," he cried, and her heart stopped cold.

Her brain flatlined, disengaging in awestruck fear. But Gabriella's voice stepped in. *"Don't react,"* it shouted. "Keep it together. He doesn't know you know. You *can't* let him know you know."

She hugged him close. She moaned, then groaned, then cried out, as his own body climaxed, before he collapsed against her.

He held her close, kissed her gently, then rose on his elbow, smoothing back her hair.

"Okay?" he asked her, tenderness laced in his tone, even as he watched her intently. He obviously realized he'd spoken her real name, and he was trying to figure out if it had registered with her.

"Fantastic," she managed with a smile, only the slightest catch to her voice.

Hot tears were building behind her eyes. But she held them at bay, snuggled up in front of him, spooning with his gorgeous, sexy, traitorous body, until his breathing went deep and even. Then her tears spilled out, dripping silently across her face to soak into the pillowcase.

Someone had obviously gotten to Sawyer.

Her enemies had found her.

Sawyer slammed the front door of his ranch house, tossing his Stetson across the room, shouting a string of the most vile swearwords in his repertoire.

Dylan instantly appeared. "What the h—?"

Sawyer swore again.

"What happened?" asked Dylan.

"I called her Niki." Sawyer could not believe he'd done it. He could not believe he had been so colossally, unforgivably stupid.

"What? When? How? What did she do?"

"Nothing," said Sawyer, still working that one through in his brain. "She didn't do anything. She didn't react. Maybe she didn't notice. Maybe she didn't hear. She might not have heard." Even as he voiced the words out loud, he had a hard time believing them.

"When? Where? What were you doing?" Dylan repeated.

Sawyer didn't answer.

"Oh," said Dylan, his flat tone conveying it all.

"I tried to resist," Sawyer felt compelled to explain. "But she's not what she's supposed to be. She's not malicious or conniving. I don't think she's plotting against anyone. From what I can tell, she's an ordinary woman in a bad circumstance, just trying to get on with her life."

"You fell for her." It wasn't a question.

Sawyer wished he could deny it. He wished he could lie. Even more than that, he wished it wasn't true.

"Of all the women in the world," Dylan drawled.

"You don't have to tell me it's bad," said Sawyer.

"What are you going to do?"

"I don't know."

Sawyer was trying to convince himself to wait and see. She'd behaved normally at breakfast, if a bit quieter than yesterday. Then again, they had made love, and slept in each other's arms last night. That could easily have changed things, made her uneasy.

On the drive home, again, there was nothing he could put his finger on. She hadn't been as carefree as she had on the river. She might have seemed distracted. But she certainly hadn't confronted him with his slip-up.

He wanted to give it a chance. He couldn't help but hope she hadn't heard him, or had been too caught up in the moment for her real name to register. More than anything, he wanted to go back to the way things were yesterday, before he'd screwed up. Not because his cover story would still be intact, but because it had been one of the best days of his life.

"If she knows you know," Dylan ventured.

"I know," Sawyer responded. "She'll be gone in a heartbeat, and I might never find her again."

He knew he should be worried about his uncle's fate. But, right now, the thought of never seeing Niki again was a stake to his heart for a whole other reason.

"Are you going to call Charles?"

"*No.* No." That was the last thing Sawyer would do.

He wasn't about to tell his uncle the romance plan was in jeopardy. He didn't want Charles or anybody else anywhere near Niki. "I'll take care of this myself."

"There's a possibility you haven't thought of," said Dylan.

"What's that?" Sawyer was open to options at this point.

"She played you."

"No."

"She knew who you were all along, and she purposely got under your skin for her own ends."

"She's not like that. She's fresh and open, kind of sweet and funny. She's intensely sexual, but in an unselfconscious way. She's not a siren."

Disbelief took over Dylan's expression. "Seriously, dude. Is that not exactly what they said about Gabriella?"

"Not in the same way." Sawyer categorically refused to believe Niki was like Gabriella. "Niki tries to differentiate herself from her mother."

But Dylan was shaking his head. "I hate to be the bearer of bad news. And please don't shoot the messenger here. But you have got to allow for the possibility that she's a great actress."

"To what end?" Sawyer demanded.

"To *this* end." Dylan gestured up and down at Sawyer. "She's got you wrapped around her little finger."

"And how does that help her?"

"I don't know," Dylan admitted. "But I bet we're going to all find out together."

"He *knows*." Niki slammed to a halt at the entrance to the living room when she noticed the room was full of people. Caleb and Mandy had arrived, and Travis seemed to be visiting.

"Who knows what?" Katrina asked, coming to her feet.

"I'm sorry," Niki hastily put in. "I didn't mean to interrupt—"

"You're not interrupting anything," Mandy quickly assured her.

Niki's gaze went to Caleb, uncertain, since they hadn't spoken since her confession. But before she could say anything, he was striding forward, pulling her into a warm embrace. "You did the right thing, little sister," he told her gruffly.

She drew back. "I wish I hadn't lied."

"Me, too. But I understand."

Niki wished she had time to appreciate Caleb and Mandy's support. But she didn't. "Sawyer knows," she repeated. "He knows I'm Niki Gerard."

"Are you sure?" asked Katrina.

"He used my real name."

"When?" asked Katrina.

Niki glanced around at the group, all eyes trained on her. "We had a nice date," she recounted, struggling to contain her embarrassment. "In a moment of inattention, he called me Niki."

"Inattention?" Reed asked, a puzzled expression on his face.

But then everybody picked up her meaning.

Travis obviously fought a smirk.

"Baby sister?" Reed chided.

"You can mock me later," she warned him.

Katrina socked her husband in the arm. "We've got a real problem here."

"I know," Reed agreed.

"What did you do?" asked Travis from where he was sitting on the sofa.

"Nothing. I pretended I didn't hear."

Reed drew back. "So, you just kept…"

Katrina hit him harder this time.

"I'm just trying to get the picture."

"We've got the picture," said Katrina. "Does he know you know?"

"I tried really hard to behave normally."

"That's impressive," Caleb put in.

"Who *is he,* then?" asked Mandy, glancing around, voicing the question that had been on Niki's mind all night. "What's he doing here? How did he find out?"

Travis pointed to the laptop on the coffee table. It showed

a photograph of Sawyer. "Here it is. He's Sawyer Layton. Nephew of Senator Charles Layton who, I'm guessing, was a former lover of Gabriella Gerard."

Niki gripped the back of an armchair. "He's from D.C.?" Then the magnitude of the situation dawned on her. "Wait a minute. He bought a ranch? He bought an entire ranch as a way to get at me."

"He got at more than just you," Caleb noted, a calm but intense anger lacing his tone. "He got more than he ever bargained for."

"He befriended us and seduced you," Reed spat, both hands curling into fists by his sides.

Niki had come to recognize that posture. Her brother was furious.

The two men gave each other a long, hard look that seemed more like a conversation.

A cold fear washed through Niki. "What are you going to—"

"Annihilate Sawyer Layton," Caleb said softly, an edge of steel to his tone.

"What?"

"They don't mean it literally," said Katrina. But then she glanced worriedly at Reed. "Right?"

"Not literally," Reed acknowledged.

Both men moved toward the door.

"Need any help?" asked Travis, coming to his feet.

"We've got it," said Reed.

"Wait!" Niki shouted.

There had to be another way. This was her problem, not theirs. She didn't want Reed and Caleb to get dragged into it any further.

"You're through hiding," Caleb told her with certainty. "Whatever this is, we're going after it head-on."

Reed stood shoulder to shoulder with his twin brother. "And 'head-on' is going to start with Sawyer Layton."

Nine

A single glance told Sawyer his cover was completely blown. Reed and Caleb's expressions were beyond grim as they made their way from their pickup truck to his ranch house.

Sawyer let the screen door bang shut behind him, took a step to the middle of the porch and braced himself.

Reed was the first to speak, hands squarely on his hips, tone a low growl in his chest. "Give me one good reason why I shouldn't take you apart."

Sawyer heard Dylan push on the screen, following him outside.

"Because," Sawyer offered reasonably, keeping his tone calm and level. "While I might not win the fight, it's going to take me a while to lose. And neither of us will feel very good when it's over."

"You son-of-a-b—"

"You want to talk about this?"

"No."

Sawyer glanced at Caleb. "We'll have to have the conversation either way. I'd rather do it before anybody starts bleeding."

Caleb's eyes were hard as coal. "You think I'm going to be more reasonable than Reed?"

"You haven't threatened me yet."

Dylan stepped up to stand next to Sawyer.

Reed's tone was icy. "You used us."

"I did," Sawyer agreed.

"You seduced our sister."

"That part's between Niki and me." Sawyer had no intention of bringing his feelings for Niki into the argument.

Caleb shook his head. "Not anymore it isn't."

Reed took a step forward. "You're going to make this go away. And then *you're* going to go away."

"I wish it were that simple," Sawyer told them honestly.

"It is that simple," said Caleb.

"I need to talk to her." Sawyer could only hope against hope that she hadn't already left town.

"That won't happen," said Reed.

"If you've seen the diary, then you know this isn't just about me."

"We know it's about your uncle."

Sawyer had always known, though he hadn't always cared, until now, that more dangerous men than his uncle would go after her. "She's got bigger problems than us."

"Not at this moment she doesn't."

The assertion gave Sawyer pause. Reed and Caleb didn't seem worried—at least, not worried enough—given the few things Sawyer knew or suspected about the identities of Gabriella's other lovers. How could they be so cavalier? And then it hit him.

"You haven't read it," he stated.

It was his turn to move closer to the Terrell brothers. He was genuinely confused. "Why haven't you read it?"

Neither of them responded.

Sawyer could feel his blood pressure rise. "You mean to

tell me *Niki* is the only one who knows who's out there gunning for her?"

It was one thing for him to be in the dark. He knew he was operating at a handicap here. But Niki's brothers should have insisted on understanding the danger. How would they have a hope in hell of helping her if they didn't even know who was after her?

The silence continued.

"She doesn't have it," Caleb admitted.

Sawyer drew back. "What?"

"She doesn't have the diary. She couldn't find it. She looked everywhere, but…"

Sawyer tried to figure out if this was a sick joke.

"Are you kidding me?" he asked. Then he marched from the porch to the ground in front of Caleb. "Are you *kidding* me?"

"There seems little reason that I would do that."

Sawyer felt a vein throb to life at his temple, and he grasped the back of his neck. "She has to find it."

"Because *you* need it?" Reed sneered.

"Because she needs it."

"You don't give a damn about my sister."

That might have been true at first, but it wasn't anymore. Sawyer did care about Niki. He cared more than made sense. Everything had turned upside down inside his head. Making her safe was his new priority.

"We want the same thing," he told Reed.

"That seems unlikely," came the man's frank reply.

"Believe me or not, but I'm on your side."

"We're going with not," said Caleb.

Sawyer nodded his acceptance. "Under the circumstances, I can't exactly blame you for that. But since you have a very big problem, and since we all know I can potentially help, you might want to find a way to reconsider."

Caleb stared levelly into his eyes. "What would make us do that?"

"I care about Niki," Sawyer told them honestly.

"Sure you do."

"Think about it," said Sawyer, deciding it was time to put his cards on the table. "I used her real name. I had an almost impenetrable cover set up here. What would cause me to make a mistake like that and use her real name?"

"That doesn't prove a thing," said Reed. He stepped closer, jabbing toward Sawyer with his index finger. "And, just so you know, I'm back to wanting to take you apart."

But Sawyer saw the hesitation in Caleb's eyes.

Caleb obviously understood that this wasn't a weakness a man wanted to admit. Who wanted to say they'd fallen so hard for a woman that they'd temporarily lost their mind while making love to her? If there wasn't so much at stake, Sawyer would have kept his mouth firmly shut on the matter.

"Tell us what you're proposing," said Caleb, earning Reed's glare of disbelief.

"We join forces," Sawyer replied.

"So you can protect your uncle?" Reed demanded.

"Niki doesn't want to hurt my uncle."

"She doesn't need money anymore," Caleb told him with conviction. "We'll make sure she never needs it again."

"She never needed money in the first place," said Sawyer. When Niki had told him the money was still there, Sawyer had investigated further. "Gabriella collected more than the two of them could spend in a dozen lifetimes. Dollars were points to her. Points in a game against powerful men. And she won every round."

"So, why is everyone afraid of Niki?"

"They think she's Gabriella. They think the game's still on."

"Tell them she's not. It's not."

"Without the diary," said Sawyer, driving home his point. "I don't know who they are."

"Hey, there." Travis's soft voice startled Niki.

A few seconds ago, she'd been alone in the living room.

Mandy and Katrina had gone upstairs with Asher, while Reed and Caleb were across the highway confronting Sawyer.

She lifted her head to watch Travis saunter in from the kitchen.

"I know what you need," he told her, a slight but clearly conspiratorial smile on his face.

"A one-way ticket to Alaska?"

"Nothing nearly so dramatic." He reached for her hand, drawing her to her feet. "You know I think of you as my sister."

She nodded. She liked that. She was growing very fond of Travis.

"But nobody else knows that's how I feel," he continued.

She didn't understand his point.

"So, I'm thinking. That you and I ought to blow this place, wander on down to the Jacobs ranch and try to take your mind off all the crap that's going on in your life. We can play ourselves a sappy, funny movie, pop some popcorn, maybe blend up a batch of strong margaritas."

"Are you asking me on a date?" The suggestion was truly baffling.

"Yeah, I am."

She squinted into his dark eyes. "Are you sick? Are you running a fever?"

"Right as rain, ma'am."

"Then, why are you talking crazy?"

"Not crazy, brilliant. I know we're only friends. And you know we're only friends. But Katrina thinks we're a pretty good match."

"That was last week."

"She won't have changed her mind this fast, trust me. Come on down to my place for a while, and I promise you, they'll stop looking at you with pity in their eyes."

Okay, now Niki got it.

"No," she told him flatly. "We are not going to pretend we're dating."

"I don't see why not. It'll give you some emotional cover until things blow over with the jerk from Washington."

She firmly shook her head. "Well, I see why not. I'm done with lying, misleading and evading. I have promised to be perfectly straight with everyone from here on in."

"That's the beauty of it," Travis noted, his eyes glinting. "We go to my place. We watch a movie, have some drinks, have some laughs, and I bring you back. Believe me, Katrina will *not* be able to resist asking you what happened."

"So, what's the point of the exercise?" Niki asked.

"The point of the exercise is, that you'll tell her the truth, that we're just friends. But she'll never believe you, not in a million years."

"You," Niki noted with a mix of incredulousness and admiration, "are really quite dangerous."

"Or you can wait here until my sisters come down." He gazed dramatically at the staircase. "And let them fuss over you for the rest of the night."

Niki's head gave an involuntary shake. She definitely wasn't in the mood to be woeful. She wanted to be strong, even if she hadn't figured out exactly how to do that yet.

"That's what I thought," said Travis. "Let's get out of here."

She held her ground a moment longer, however, she could hear Mandy and Katrina moving upstairs. They'd be back down in a minute, and Niki really didn't want to face their well-intentioned sympathy.

"You don't have to do this," she told him, even as she retrieved her purse and a sweater.

"I'm a little bored," he returned easily, silently opening the front door and gesturing for her to exit first. "I figure a chick flick is better than sitting around here with the old, married people."

"Liar," she accused, following his lead to a nearby pickup truck.

"Really? After your little caper this summer, you want to throw stones at my honesty?"

Niki clamped her mouth shut.

"That's more like it." He held the door open while she climbed in.

But as he hopped in the driver's side, his expression turned sober. "You know, you're going to come through this."

She managed a nod, but she didn't deserve his help, nor the kindness of these two families. Yet she couldn't seem to stop herself from accepting it. She reached out to Travis's hand on the stick shift, squeezing thanks as he pulled in a tight circle to head down the driveway.

The evening went by thankfully fast. By the end of the funny movie and her second jumbo golden margarita, Niki felt a whole lot better about life. Travis ferried her back to the Terrell ranch, helping her out of the truck and up the stairs to the porch. She wasn't exactly unsteady on her feet, but her head was definitely lighter than usual. Tequila, she decided, was a very good antidote for heartache.

Outside the front door, he stopped, turning her and placing his hands loosely on her shoulders.

"Remember," he told her. "You're only obligated to tell the truth. It's up to everyone else to interpret it."

She scoffed out a laugh, giving a soft hiccup to go with it. "I'm sure glad you're on my side," she told him.

He pulled her into a brief hug, giving her a quick peck on the cheek and rubbing his palms along her upper arms. "I'll always be on your side, Niki." Then he pushed open the door, stepped aside to let her go forward.

She pivoted and came face-to-face with Sawyer, the unexpected sight of him causing her to stumble, and her knees to nearly give out in shock.

His angry gaze shot straight past her, settling on Travis.

"What are you—?" Niki sputtered. What was Sawyer doing in the Terrell house?

"I could ask you the same thing." His hard gaze was still trained on Travis.

"We were at my place," Travis put in amicably, not seeming the least bit intimidated. "Together. Taking in a movie."

Niki could have kissed him for shielding her pride in the face of Sawyer. She was an instant and eternal fan of his devious ways.

"We had margaritas," she added for good measure.

Sawyer's attention returned to her. "I have to talk to you."

"Not a good time," she answered airily. She waggled her fingertips in a wave as she slipped past him.

Travis's footsteps followed her inside. Rounding the corner into the living room, she found her two brothers.

"Oh, good," she breathed. "You're both here."

"What did you do to her?" asked Reed, but there didn't seem to be any anger in his tone.

"Nothing," Travis answered, tracking after her into the room. "We're just friends."

Niki snickered. She turned to face him, wagging an admonishing finger in front of his face. "You are very, very good."

Humor flashed through his eyes. "Thank you. You're not so bad yourself."

"What the hell?" asked Caleb in obvious confusion, as Sawyer took up a position near the window, clearly fuming.

Niki turned to face Caleb again. "We're just friends. Now, what is *he* doing here?" She frowned, jabbing a thumb in Sawyer's direction. "I thought you were going to annihilate him."

"We changed our minds," replied Caleb.

"That's really too bad because he's a cad and a liar."

"Can we talk?" Sawyer asked her.

Niki fought against the wave of hurt and regret sweeping through her. She tilted her chin. "There's nothing left to say."

But her light-headedness was evaporating, and along with it the numbing effects of the tequila. She was starting to feel sick to her stomach.

"I want to help," Sawyer told her.

"Do I look stupid?" She glanced accusingly at Reed and Caleb. "How'd he get in here?"

"You should listen to him," said Caleb.

"I'm still on the fence about that," said Reed.

"I can take you back to my place again," Travis offered.

"Back off," Sawyer barked at him, dark eyes glittering with anger.

"We're just friends," she repeated, wondering why she even bothered. Friends or more, it was none of Sawyer's business. It had never been any of his business.

"Can this wait until morning?" she asked no one in particular.

"You have to go back to D.C.," Sawyer told her.

She rounded on him. "Are you going to tie me up and thme in a trunk?"

"Tempting."

"This is getting us nowhere," Caleb put in. "Niki, how drunk are you?"

"I'm not drunk."

"She's not drunk," Travis echoed.

"Is that what you're telling yourself?" Sawyer challenged him.

"Really?" Travis took a step toward Sawyer. "Seriously? *You're* going to lecture *me?*"

"Time out," Caleb called, making a T sign with his two hands. "Niki, Sawyer wants to help you find the diary."

"Certainly he does." Her head was spinning just enough to be disorienting.

Sawyer would help her find the diary, and then he'd take it from her and hand it over to his family.

Gabriella had warned her they'd come after it. It didn't take a rocket scientist to figure out that Sawyer's uncle was in the diary. Gabriella had made it clear the diary was Niki's ace in the hole, and she should protect it from all comers.

"Nobody gets the diary," she told Sawyer with conviction.

His tone went softer as he spoke to her. "Many people will try."

"They won't find it."

"That's not the point. They're terrified of you, Niki. They'll hunt you until they find *you*."

"Like you did?" she challenged.

"Like I did," he admitted. "I was the first, but I won't be the last. You're in trouble."

"Because of *you*," she couldn't help pointing out.

"Not anymore. I'm on your side now."

Niki looked to Caleb. Over the past few months, she learned ~~s~~ cool and smart in any circumstance.

~~)~~ you trust him?" she asked.

~~I~~ come to D.C. with you," Caleb told her.

~~Y~~ou can't," said Sawyer.

Caleb's lips tightened in a frown.

"If they see you with her, her safety net is gone. Until we straighten this out, nobody can connect Niki with the Terrells."

"Then, I'll go," said Travis.

"Same problem," Sawyer returned.

Travis squared his shoulders. "Well, we're not entrusting her to you alone."

Niki was beginning to feel like a prize in a tug-of-war. "Can we please stop?" This argument was getting them nowhere.

"Have you read the diary?" Sawyer asked her.

"No." The only reason she told him the truth was because she was sick and tired of lying. It wasn't because she owed him anything.

He took a few steps toward her. "Here's the thing. They know who you are, but you don't know who they are. Step one, is to identify them. To do that, we have to read the diary."

"There is no 'we.'" Though she didn't disagree with the rest of it. She needed to put names to these former lovers of Gabriella's.

"I know D.C.," Sawyer offered reasonably. "I know the city, and I know the players. I can keep you safe there."

"I don't need your help." She wanted to get out from under this threat. But she didn't want anything more to do with Sawyer.

Instead of answering her, he looked to Caleb, Reed and then Travis, setting his gaze on each of them. "If I hurt her in any way, I know you'll come after me."

"Damn straight," said Reed.

"And I have complete faith in your ability to annihilate me."

"Don't doubt it for a second," said Travis.

"Does anybody care what I think?" As Niki glanced from man to man, she realized they didn't. The living room contained more testosterone than the Giants starting lineup.

"Fine." She agreed. Though she wasn't giving in. Instead, she was taking control.

The threat was in Washington, and to Washington she would go.

Niki watched the clouds slip past below them from the window of Caleb's private jet. She understood the wisdom of not traveling on a commercial airline, but she hated being cooped up all alone with Sawyer for hours. She wished she'd thought to tell him to take a commercial flight, coach, an inside seat with screaming toddlers on either side.

Reed probably would have gone for it. Then again, given what she'd learned about the Layton family, Sawyer would have simply called in his own jet. That might have kept him away from Niki, but it would have done nothing for her revenge fantasy.

"You feeling okay?" Sawyer asked, breaking the silence that had stretched for over half an hour. He was in a seat on the opposite side of the eight passenger jet, one row ahead.

"I'm not speaking to you," she informed him.

He turned. "You seemed a little tipsy last night. I was worried you might be hungover."

"That's none of your business." She'd been slightly tipsy after the margaritas, and she was a little wooly this morning, but that was hardly a federal crime.

"I didn't mean to hurt you," he repeated to her.

"You didn't," she told him airily. "You embarrassed yourself."

He was silent for a moment. "We both know that's not true."

She looked at him for the first time. "Do we? I'm the one who took pity on you and faked it."

A muscle flexed in the side of his cheek. "I was pretty sure you had to have heard me."

"When you called me Niki?" She forced out a laugh. "Yeah, I recognized my own name."

"If you hadn't—never mind. Stupid question. I'm having a car meet us at the airport."

"Whatever." She waved a dismissive hand.

She'd thought long and hard overnight, scrambling for new ideas of where the diary might be hidden. But there was simply no place left to look.

Maybe if she'd been thinking more clearly last night, she could have articulated that logic. But that chance was gone, and she was here, and she was going to have to suffer through Sawyer's company for the next couple of days.

"We have to stop at the Layton mansion."

Sawyer's words took her by surprise.

"I'm not going anywhere near that place." Charles Layton was apparently one of her most powerful enemies. She sure wasn't delivering herself into his hands.

"It won't take me long," said Sawyer. "There's a guest house I use. You can't even see the mansion from there."

"Drop me off somewhere first."

"There's nowhere safe."

"A restaurant? A hotel?"

"I'm not dropping you off in a public place. And I'm definitely not leaving you on your own. We don't know who's watching for you, and where they might be."

"Nobody will recognize me dressed like this." Never mind the new hair color and glasses, she'd dressed in plain jeans, a pink tank top and a roomy, white hoodie, that camouflaged most everything, including her face when the hood was up.

"That's not a risk I'm willing to take."

"It's a risk I'm willing to take. And it's my choice, Sawyer."

"He'll never know you're there."

"Was this your plot from the start?" she demanded, her imagination suddenly taking flight, causing her to seriously question the wisdom of trusting him at all. "Are you kidnapping me?"

Was she going to appear on the evening news? A recent picture, maybe from last year's cotillion flashing on the screen while the announcer talked about Gabriella's death and Niki's subsequent disappearance or murder?

Her stomach churned with a wave of anxiety.

"Don't be ridiculous," Sawyer responded.

"I won't go quietly," she warned him.

When they exited the airplane, would there be time to flee? Would he have armed guards to meet them? Would they gag her and toss her in the backseat of a car?

"Whatever you're thinking," Sawyer intoned. "Stop."

"Are you truly evil?"

"No."

"I think you are."

"I'm not."

"I think you're going to kill me and take your chances with Reed and Caleb. How will you get away from them, Sawyer? Do you own a secret Caribbean island?"

"Do you need a drink?"

"I'm not letting you get me drunk."

He gazed at the ceiling in what looked like a prayer for patience. "You are perfectly safe, Niki."

"I'm in a lot of danger," she retorted.

"Yeah, well, that may be true. But you're not in danger from me."

"We both know you're a liar."

He laughed at that, reminding her of why she'd been attracted to him. "And we both know you're pure of heart?"

"I never blackmailed anyone. And neither did my mother."

Her stomach was beginning to calm down. She realized she couldn't bring herself to believe Sawyer was a coldhearted killer.

"We'll know for sure once we read the diary," he said.

"I don't think we'll find it."

"You probably want to start thinking about places to look."

"I've looked everywhere."

"If you'd looked everywhere, you'd have found it," he offered calmly.

His cool reasoning made her mad.

"I'm not speaking to you," she reminded him.

"I can tell."

She pressed her lips together. If he wasn't so insufferable, she might be able to keep silent. Still, if she didn't speak up for herself and her mother in all this, who would?

"Why do you want to go to your mansion?"

Sawyer glanced laconically at his watch. "You lasted exactly twenty-five seconds."

"Shut up."

"I can shut up, or I can answer your question, but you're going to have to choose."

"I have a lot at stake," she defended.

"I never said otherwise."

She sucked in a steadying breath. "*Why* do you want to go to your mansion?"

"Because, if I show up in D.C., and I don't stop to see Charles, he'll get suspicious."

"Are you planning on telling him that you found me?"

"He already knows I found you."

"Does he know your cover's blown?"

"No."

"Will you tell him that?"

"No." Sawyer paused. "Luckily for you, I'm a damn fine liar."

"Did he help you buy the ranch?" She had spent the last day

and a half trying to wrap her head around Sawyer purchasing an entire cattle ranch as a cover story.

"I bought the ranch."

"I can't understand the super rich."

"You can't understand yourself?"

"I'm not superrich." She knew Gabriella had been very well off. But she couldn't approach the inter-generational wealth of people like the Laytons.

"Have you checked your Swiss bank account lately?" Sawyer asked.

"I haven't had time. And how do you know she had a Swiss bank account?"

"I can afford good investigators."

Pain was beginning to throb to life at the base of Niki's neck. She closed her eyes and leaned back against the white leather seat. "If you people know I have money," she said, enjoying the darkness. "Why do you think I'd resort to blackmail?"

"Nobody thinks you want money, Niki." Sawyer's deep voice seemed to surround her, and her name on his lips sent a deep shiver along her spine. "They think you want power."

"Tell them I don't."

"I will. Just as soon as we find out who they are."

Ten

It was a straightforward matter to get Niki into the guest house. He had been sneaking in and out of it, at all hours of the day and night, with or without company, since he was sixteen years old.

As a teenager, he'd commandeered the little house and customized it to his tastes. Though he now spent most of his time in his own penthouse in Georgetown, he still often stayed over.

"You'll be safe here," he found himself telling Niki as he pulled the suite door shut behind him. Once he'd uttered the words, he realized they sounded overly dramatic.

She glanced from the hunter-green wraparound sofa, out the view window that overlooked the grounds and the public golf course beyond, to the narrow, wrought-iron staircase that led to his loft bedroom.

"Bathroom is through that door," he told her. "I hope you're not too hungry."

They hadn't eaten anything on the plane, and he had nothing to offer her here. Hopefully, he could get away from his uncle fairly quickly, and they could rustle up a meal.

"I'll survive," she told him, wandering toward the window. "As long as you're not planning to kill me off to keep me quiet."

"Not today," said Sawyer.

"Comforting."

He moved up behind her. "Tell me you're not truly frightened." He couldn't stand it if she was.

"I don't know what to think. I don't know what to expect. Since the day my mother died, I've been jumpy and anxious, and I'd love to know how to make it stop."

He touched her shoulder, but she shrugged away.

He let his hand drop back to his side. "I'm trying to help you."

"So, you've said." She turned. "But your priority is your own family, and I'm a threat to them."

Sawyer didn't know how to respond. She was a threat to his family. But that didn't mean he didn't care about her. She was as much a victim in this as anyone, maybe more so. Gabriella might have catalogued those men's secrets, but the men were the ones who'd stepped out of line to begin with.

Niki had never stepped out of line. She hadn't picked her mother. Fate had done that for her.

"I'll be as quick as I can," he told her.

She simply shrugged in return. "I'll be here."

He hesitated. "You won't try anything stupid, will you? Don't leave, Niki. I'm your best hope."

"You're my worst nightmare." She looked sexy, vulnerable, compelling to the extreme.

He had to fight to keep from pulling her into his arms. "If it wasn't me, it would be someone else."

"Is that how you sleep at night?"

There were times in his life when he didn't sleep much at all. And this was one of those times. There was no good answer here. No way for everyone to win. But he'd vowed to himself that Niki wouldn't be the loser.

"Wait here," he pleaded. "Just...wait for me."

He left her then, praying she'd do the smart thing.

He drove the main driveway, parking out front and mounting the wide, semicircle staircase to the entry foyer. There, he took a short hallway along the front of the mansion to his uncle's home office. Sawyer had checked earlier and learned Charles would be working from the mansion.

Charles's assistant Kelly showed no surprise at Sawyer's appearance.

"He's inside reading," Kelly told him. "Go on in."

Sawyer pushed open the oversized oak door, finding his uncle behind a massive cherry wood desk. The windows were ajar, allowing a breeze to waft across the rose garden, partially dissipating the scent of old leather.

Charles looked up, peering over the top of his reading glasses. "What are *you* doing here?" he demanded without preamble. "If you found it, you should have called right away."

"I haven't found it."

"Then get your ass back to Colorado. I don't care if you're sick of cow dung and black flies."

"I'm not sick of Colorado," said Sawyer. "I'm staying in D.C. for a few days. Check things out from this end."

"Niki Gerard's not here," his uncle said flatly, setting down the report and removing his glasses. "You can't make her fall for you if you're not even in the same state."

"Well, the diary is not in Colorado," Sawyer countered.

Charles squinted, deepening the wrinkles around his eyes. "You know that for a fact?"

"I know that for a fact."

"How?"

Sawyer helped himself to a caramel candy from the small dish at the edge of the ornate desk. "Leave the details to me."

"I want to know what's going on."

"Want and need are two different things." Sawyer pulled on the ends of the wrapper, untwisting the gold foil.

Charles paused, his brain obviously sorting through the information. "Are you saying it's better if I don't know?"

"It's better if you don't know," Sawyer echoed. It was better for Niki, rather than Charles, but Sawyer felt no compulsion to add that information to the mix.

"Hans Koeper has been calling," said Charles.

Sawyer went on alert. "Asking about the diary?"

"His questions were oblique, but I think we can count him amongst the lucky winners of the Gabriella lottery."

"Does it bother you—" Sawyer stopped himself.

"That she slept with other men?" Charles finished. "That was a long time ago, Sawyer. And she was never a long-term proposition. What bothers me is that it might come back to haunt me."

"You know about anyone else?" Sawyer asked.

"Other than Harbottle, Carter and my suspicions about Newlin? Nothing new from my sources."

Sawyer sat down in one of the two guest chairs positioned to face Charles's desk. "You ever think she might not do anything?" he asked.

"Who might not do anything?"

"Niki Gerard." Sawyer watched his uncle's expression carefully. "She hasn't made any move so far, except to run away to Colorado. She might want to put this all behind her."

"You've been hanging around Midwesterners too long."

"Not everyone in D.C. is dishonest."

"Everyone in D.C. has an angle. Nobody throws away that kind of leverage."

"Niki would."

Charles sat up. "What do you mean Niki would? How would you know that? What aren't you telling me?"

"I'm telling you the woman I met in Colorado seems to want to stay there and live a quiet life."

"She's lying about her identity."

"True," Sawyer was forced to agree.

"She's laying low and biding her time."

"Or, she's trying to leave the past behind."

Charles's voice boomed in anger. "You don't know these women."

"You only knew one of them," Sawyer countered.

"I know human nature," said Charles. "Now, quit second-guessing me and do your job."

It was nearly five o'clock when Sawyer made it back to the guest house. His sister and her fiancé had dropped by and caught him as he was leaving Charles's office. They wanted to bring him up to speed on their wedding plans, and there was no plausible reason for him not to stay and talk.

Afterward, starving, and assuming Niki must be feeling the same way, he stopped by the kitchen and loaded up with a couple of sandwiches, some plums and a bottle of wine.

Now, he entered the cottage and found it quiet. He paused in the doorway, noting it was far too quiet.

He could have kicked himself for staying away so long, or maybe for having left Niki alone in the first place. Although he couldn't imagine any reasonable person running off on her own through D.C. under the circumstances. He knew she was operating on emotion and adrenaline, rather than reason, at the moment.

He moved farther into the room to set down the food, and there he saw her. She was on the sofa, lying on her side, legs curled up, with her head on the mini plaid pillow. The tension evaporated from his body, and he moved automatically toward her.

"Niki?" he asked softly, not wanting to startle her.

She didn't stir.

On the coffee table, he placed the things he'd been carrying, coming down on one knee. "Niki?"

Still nothing.

It occurred to him that he should leave her sleeping. It wasn't like they had to rush off anywhere.

He gazed at her beautiful face for several minutes. Her cheeks were flushed, lashes lush against her skin, her red lips were slightly parted, and her hair was sexily mussed across her forehead.

The only thing marring the picture were her glasses, which were slightly askew. He gently lifted them away from her face, folding them, then reaching over her to set them on the side table.

Her eyes fluttered open.

"Hi," she said sleepily, a slight smile turning up her lips.

"Hi, yourself," he returned, fighting an almost compulsive urge to cradle her face and kiss her mouth.

"I fell asleep," she told him, the tone of her voice ratcheting up the powerful emotions in his chest.

"You did," he agreed, the urge to kiss her strengthening by the second.

He met the soft green of her eyes and felt the tiny puff of her breath. His hand lifted, thumb touching the soft flush of her cheek.

"Good morning, beautiful," he whispered, his lips going down on hers.

She kissed him back, and it lasted a sweet, sexy, extraordinarily satisfying three seconds.

But then she jerked back. "What are you *doing?*"

"I'm sorry." But he wasn't.

She glanced around, pulling herself into a sitting position, wedging her knees protectively between them. "How long have I been asleep? What time is it?"

"It's five o'clock."

She stared at him. "You can't kiss me, Sawyer."

"I know."

"You should never have kissed me in the first place."

"I tried to stop," he told her in all honesty.

"Yeah, right."

"You know I tried." He touched her arm, but she jerked away.

He did a quick mental debate, telling himself to leave it alone, but he found he couldn't. "That first day in the river, it was me that pulled back. When we made love in the hotel room, I tried to say no. This thing with you and me was never part of the plan."

Her expression faltered, and he knew she remembered.

"I didn't plan on being attracted to you. I couldn't help myself."

Her brows went up. "Is that supposed to be a compliment?"

"I swear to you I tried to keep it under control, but every time you looked at me, I wanted you. And when you kissed me, wrapped your arms around me, pressed against me, there was no way I could stop myself."

"Please tell me you're not looking for sympathy."

He waited a beat before continuing. "Maybe I am. Maybe I'm looking for understanding. Because I still like you, Niki. And I still want you. And I know I'm making compromises to what I'm supposed to be doing, because of my feelings for you."

"You're making compromises because you got caught, Sawyer."

"Getting caught is not my biggest problem."

His biggest problem was the fact that he cared more about saving Niki than he did about protecting his family. The whole situation was a colossal conflict of interest. But he had no desire or intention to step away.

Even if she didn't know it, Niki needed him. And he wasn't going to abandon her. He was going to extricate her from this web of conflict and treachery, or go down trying.

"I'm still attracted to you," he confessed. "And it's messing with my concentration."

Her shoulders relaxed ever so slightly. "You do know I'd be a fool to believe you."

"You're not a fool, Niki Gerard."

"And I don't believe you."

He cocked his head to one side, thinking about kissing her all over again. "Doesn't mean it's not true."

"Stop," she ordered.

"Are you hungry? I brought sandwiches and wine."

She glanced past him to the food he'd laid on the table. "I'm hungry," she admitted.

"We can eat first and fight later," he offered.

"This fight is over. I won. Move on, Sawyer."

He couldn't help but smile. "You're attracted to me, Niki. You might as well come clean on that."

"I was attracted to Sawyer Smith, gentleman rancher. I have zero interest in Sawyer Layton, lying, scheming, D.C. operative."

"We're the same guy."

She shook her head. "Only one of you will ever sleep with me."

"Oh, darlin'," Sawyer couldn't seem to stop himself from drawling. "You don't want to be throwing down a challenge like that."

Though Niki hated to admit Sawyer was right, he was right. Sawyer Smith and Sawyer Layton were the same person, and she was attracted to him, more attracted than ever now that she knew she couldn't have him.

They'd left the guest house soon after eating and spent the night in his Georgetown penthouse. He had a massive apartment, taking up the entire top floor of an eighteen-story building overlooking Waterfront Park. It had three bedrooms. She'd taken the one farthest from the master, not wanting to think about Sawyer on the other side of a wall for the entire night.

This morning, his housekeeper had prepared omelets and provided fresh bagels from a neighborhood bakery. Niki and Sawyer sat on his veranda, breathing the fresh breeze, watching pedestrians along the walkway, hearing the hum of traffic in the distance, interspersed with the occasional blast of a horn.

"Is there a safe in your apartment?" Sawyer was asking. "A hidden compartment? Maybe something you didn't know about?"

Niki shook her head as she bit into a blueberry bagel. "I

looked behind every picture, behind the furniture, under the beds, under the rugs."

The conversation reminded her of how baffled she'd felt in the days before she fled to Colorado.

"Weird thing is," she told Sawyer. "She wanted me to find it. She talked about it just before she died. She told me it would keep me safe. There's no way she purposefully hid it from me. I swear, she thought I'd know where to look."

Sawyer sat back. "So, somewhere simple, somewhere straightforward. In plain sight?"

"It wasn't beside her bed, or in a magazine rack, or in a desk drawer."

"Safe-deposit box?"

"I thought of that, too. I've been over all the papers with the lawyers. The only place I didn't look was in Switzerland. But why would she keep the diary in Switzerland?"

"You want to pop over there and find out?"

Niki couldn't stifle her grin. "You know, I led a fairly opulent lifestyle with Gabriella. Beach resorts in Tahiti, skiing in St. Moritz—"

"You ski?"

"I snowboard. But that's not the point."

"I don't know why that surprises me."

"I also do a little dressage, sail and golf."

His gaze turned speculative. "You're very sporty."

"So?" Where was this getting them?

"I was thinking you'd be a whole lot of fun on vacation."

"Sawyer, stop."

"What? A guy can't dream?"

"No, a guy can't dream."

"Have you played golf at Wailea?"

"No. I don't think so. I don't remember."

"It's on Maui. You'd probably remember if you'd ever been there."

"Not if I was nine years old. I've been golfing for a while.

It gave my mother an excuse to buy memberships at exclusive country clubs."

"She didn't play?"

"What?" Niki couldn't help but smile at that. "Get windblown? Break a sweat? Gabriella struck a pose a whole lot better inside the clubhouse than out on the fairway."

Sawyer smiled in response. "We should do Wailea."

"We're not dating," she pointed out.

"You can have your own room."

"We've got work to do here. I don't think we should be taking a golf trip."

Sawyer set down his coffee cup. "That is another approach, you know."

"Another approach to what?"

"We get out of here?"

"Out of your penthouse?" Niki didn't understand. Was he suggesting they start combing the city for her mother's diary?

"Out of D.C. Out of the country. We take a world tour and never come back."

If it was just a matter of leaving D.C., Niki could have seen herself doing it. Not necessarily with Sawyer, of course. But maybe on her own, just run away and never come back.

But there was Colorado to think about now. She wasn't willing to give up her brothers, or her sisters-in-law, her little nephew. If it came down to fight or flee, this time she was staying to fight.

Niki pushed away her plate. "I need to take a shower now. Let me know if you come up with a serious idea."

"I am serious." He looked dead serious.

"Wait a minute." Niki suddenly felt as if she'd been struck by a bolt of lightning.

"Is that a yes?" Sawyer asked, brightening.

"The Congressional Country Club."

Sawyer hesitated. "Sure. We can golf there, if you want. Not much of a trip though, and a whole lot of people who might know you."

Niki leaned forward. "We were members."

"Well, that doesn't surprise me, given your mother's apparent political connections."

"I golfed. My mother didn't. She preferred the various public and private rooms of the clubhouse. We had a locker." Niki stopped talking.

Sawyer obviously felt the same lightning bolt. "You had—*have* a locker."

Niki nodded.

"And she would have expected you to go there."

"Yes."

"Open the locker."

"Yes."

"She never expected you to spend three months in Colorado."

"Now, you're catching on."

"Oh, I've caught completely on. How long will it take you to get ready?"

"Give me thirty minutes."

Niki showered, dried her hair and put on some makeup. Unfortunately, she had nothing suitable to wear to the club. Her hair and glasses created a partial disguise. And she could add a hat and scarf, but the less she stood out, the better.

A quick trip to a boutique down the block had her outfitted in a cowl-neck white sleeveless sweater, a short pleated plaid skirt, a pair of navy flats, and a floppy hat and colorful silk scarf that partially obscured her face.

In the foyer of his penthouse, Sawyer eyed her critically. "It's really hard to dress you down."

"I'm trying to blend," she pointed out.

"Thank goodness for the glasses."

"You don't like my glasses?" Niki had gotten used to them and was growing quite fond of them.

"I love your glasses. I love the outfit. I think you look sensational."

"What's your point?"

"My point is you'll attract attention wherever you go."

Niki's hands went to her hips. "Why? I don't understand." She glanced in the hallway mirror. "I look perfectly ordinary."

"You look like a sex kitten trying to pretend she's a librarian."

"Excuse me?"

"In an odd kind of way, it makes you sexier."

"You're being ridiculous."

"Why do you think your mother was so successful?"

"I know she was pretty," Niki admitted. There was no point in pretending anything else.

"She was beyond pretty. She was the kind of woman men meet and then fantasize about for the rest of their lives."

Niki frowned. "You're talking about my mother here."

"But I'm thinking about you. I don't know what you see when you look in the mirror, but I see intense bedroom eyes, flushed cheeks and pouty lips with a just-loved swollen look that drives a man out of his mind. Right now, it's all I can do not to haul you into the nearest bedroom, throw up that flirty, little skirt and ravish you on the spot."

Niki was literally speechless. She was also intensely aroused, and completely unnerved by her reaction to him. What on earth did a woman say in response to that?

Besides yes. And, oh, how she wanted to say yes.

"Don't look at me like that," Sawyer growled.

"I'm…not…"

He took a step toward her, then another.

As his hands spanned her rib cage, she told herself to protest. But they were warm through her sweater, sexy, arousing. Her backed her up, deliberately, relentlessly, until she was pressed up against the wall.

Then in slow motion, giving her plenty of time to say no, he bent to kiss her. He planted his mouth firmly against her own, engulfing her lips, his tongue invading, his arms sliding around her.

She moaned once before her arms twined around his neck.

She came up on her toes, tipped her head, deepened their kiss, letting her passion run wild through her bloodstream. This was a terrible, terrible idea, but, she'd wanted him for so long.

He kissed her neck, pulled aside the sweater, kissing his way to her bare shoulder. One hand encircled her breast, and she felt her nipple peak instantly against his palm.

She moaned his name, her fingers digging into his hair, bracing herself against the smooth, solid wall.

"Niki," he groaned. This time, her name on his lips brought nothing but a massive wave of desire that took over her system, hijacking her last shred of reason.

His free hand found the hem of her skirt, fingers contacting her bare leg. He stroked upward, and her breathing deepened. Then he found the silken scrap of her panties.

"Do you want this?" he growled in her ear.

"Yes," she hissed in abject surrender. "Yes."

He stripped off her panties, tossing them aside. Then he swiftly loosened his own pants, producing a condom, lifting her, wrapping her legs around his waist.

"Okay?" he asked breathlessly.

She gave a rapid nod, biting down on her bottom lip to keep from begging him to do it, to make them one again.

He thrust inside.

She buried her face in the crook of his neck, tasting the salt of his skin, inhaling his musky scent, tightening her thighs around him as he moved rhythmically in and out.

His hands were hot on her buttocks, the wall cool against her back. His lips found hers again, drinking deeply, his tongue demanding, while his body took her to higher and higher heights.

She seemed to shimmer forever, sounds ringing in her ears, lights flashing before her eyes, muscles clenching harder and harder. Then he called out her name, and the world cascaded into ecstasy.

After long minutes, her body's throbbing subsided. Their breathing seemed to stabilize. Sawyer slowly turned, bracing his own back against the wall. Then he sank down, and her legs touched the soft carpet, and he came to a rest.

He gave her a sweet kiss, then touched his forehead to hers.

Her pleasure was rapidly being replaced by embarrassment. What had she done? What had they done? A romantic date ending in the bed of a fine hotel was one thing. But this was a quick, lusty interlude in his hallway, when they knew better, when they should have kept their hands completely to themselves.

When she managed to speak, her voice sounded small. "I don't suppose we could forget this ever happened?"

"We can try." His tone was decidedly skeptical.

"How about we make sure it never happens again?"

"We can try." He tipped his head and kissed her mouth, then again, and again.

She drew in a heavy, heady breath. "I'm not liking our chances much," she admitted.

He smoothed back her hair, gazing softly into her eyes. "Let's just get through today, okay? Then we'll see what happens after that."

"This would be so much easier if you were evil."

"I was thinking exactly the same thing about you."

Eleven

After Sawyer signed them into the Congressional Country Club, Niki started on the most direct route to the locker room. They made it through the lobby, down the main staircase and along the breezeway that bypassed the signature restaurant and the cigar lounge.

But, cutting across a veranda, their luck ran out.

"Sawyer," a thirty-ish man boomed. His hair was trimmed neat. He wore a dark suit, white shirt, silk tie and expensive wingtips.

"Miles," Sawyer answered smoothly, giving the man a handshake. "Good to see you again so soon."

Miles glanced curiously at Niki.

"This is Nellie," said Sawyer. "An…acquaintance of mine. We met in St. Moritz a few years back."

The expression on Miles's face would have been insulting if it wasn't so convenient. Clearly, he thought acquaintance was a euphemism for one-night stand.

"Nellie," Sawyer continued. "Miles is a Congressman from Delaware. He's engaged to my sister Roxanne."

"Pleasure to meet you," said Niki. "I, uh, need to…" She gestured vaguely in the direction of the veranda staircase.

"Please, join me." Miles indicated a nearby table.

"We were on our way out," said Sawyer. "She's got a plane to catch."

Miles nodded knowingly, sliding a glance at Niki. Fortunately, he was paying very little attention to her face. "Nuff said."

Sawyer clapped him on the shoulder. "Appreciate your discretion."

"Not a problem."

Then Sawyer swiftly guided Niki toward the stairs.

"Lovely," she muttered under her breath.

"Ensures he won't ask any questions about you around my family. He thinks he's in on a dirty little secret."

"I've never been anyone's dirty little secret."

"You're turning me on."

"That's disgusting."

Sawyer grinned unrepentantly.

"Layton," came another voice. This one from a sixty-something man, also dressed in an expensive suit, which only made sense, given there was no one here but the who's who of the city.

"Judge Needly," Sawyer responded with the obligatory handshake.

The man barely glanced at Niki, clearly dismissing her as unimportant. Fine with her.

"How's your uncle?" Judge Needly asked.

"Doing well," said Sawyer.

Niki took a slow step backward, keeping her head turned, glancing surreptitiously around to see if she recognized anyone seated at the tables. She wondered if she should keep walking by herself. At this rate, she and Sawyer were never going to make it to the locker room, let alone back out of the club again.

The judge leaned in to Sawyer. "I hear through the grapevine that Charles and I may have a mutual interest."

"Sir?" Sawyer asked.

"A little issue that came up about three months ago. A matter requiring a certain amount of confidentiality."

Niki keyed in on the conversation. About three months ago? She glanced at Sawyer, but his face remained impassive.

"Is there a way I can help?" Sawyer asked.

Judge Needly kept his voice low. "I know Charles is involved." He held up his hand. "No, no. Don't bother confirming or denying. My sources are solid. Just tell Charles to give me a call when he has a chance. I've got a few things in the works that might interest him."

"I'll tell him," said Sawyer. Again, his expression betrayed nothing.

"Appreciate it," said the judge, offering another handshake.

"Not at all," Sawyer returned.

Once again, she and Sawyer went on their way.

"What is the matter with you people?" Niki demanded.

"Who people? Club members?"

"Men," she clarified. "Is there some unspoken fraternity of illicit sex amongst you rich guys?"

"Pretty much," said Sawyer.

She stared at him in shocked disbelief.

He shrugged. "What do you want me to say? Many women are attracted to wealth and power. Some powerful men take advantage of the situation."

"No wonder you're so easy to manipulate."

"Hey." He held his palms up in surrender. "I'm not the guy doing it."

"You let Miles think you were."

"That was to protect you, not me." His arm slipped around her shoulders, and for a split second she allowed herself to feel safe.

They made it to the bottom of the stairs.

"We can't talk about it now," said Sawyer as they approached the outside entrance to the locker room. "But I'd never be anything but proud to show you off as mine."

She shrugged her way out of his embrace. "You mean if things were different?"

"That's not what I—"

"Things aren't different, Sawyer. And they're never going to be different. I think we should stick to our original agreement." She had to keep a firm grip on reality here. Falling for Sawyer had hurt her once. She couldn't let it happen again.

"What was that?"

"We forget it happened."

"I didn't—"

"Look, ladies only." She pushed open the locker-room door and left him standing outside.

Inside, the locker room was exactly how Niki remembered it. It had been quite some time since she'd been here, although the place was as serene and quiet as always. Pastel armchairs formed comfortable groupings in a parlor area. Outside the restrooms were several makeup tables, complete with upholstered, French provincial chairs. Floral arrangements were placed on polished glass tables, and baskets of expensive toiletries were displayed along gleaming, marble counters.

A large archway led to the locker area. No gray, utilitarian metal here. They were Maplewood closets, covered in a smooth, satin finish, arranged in neat rows, with crown molding along the top. There was a richly padded bench stretching down the middle of the aisle.

Niki stopped at number sixty-one. It was a corner unit, slightly larger than most others. She dialed the combination and opened the louvered door. Inside was a row of hangers with a single sweater she'd left behind the last time she'd played. On the floor of the locker were two pairs of golf shoes. And on the top shelf, there was a makeup bag and a couple of bottles of shampoo and conditioner.

She went up on her toes, feeling around at the back of the shelf. Her hand contacted a second makeup case. She drew it forward. It was turquoise leather, with a jeweled zipper and two front pockets. Niki had never seen it before.

She glanced over each shoulder, confirming she was still alone. She drew the zipper slowly open, holding her breath, hardly believing she might have actually found it.

Sure enough. There it was, a thick, tan leather volume with parchment pages, each covered in her mother's flowery handwriting. Niki couldn't help but smile as she flipped through and saw the different colored ink. Her mother had written in pink, purple, red, green and orange.

Impulsively, she raised the open book to her nose and inhaled. It was Gabriella's perfume, and Niki had to blink back tears.

"Oh, mom." She sighed. "I wish I was as brave as you."

But Gabriella's voice was silent inside her head. This was obviously new territory for both of them.

Niki zipped up the turquoise case, shut the locker door and secured it. Then she squared her shoulders, retracing her steps, opening the outside door to meet Sawyer's quizzical gaze.

She discreetly pointed to the case, receiving a slight nod in return. Then he took her arm, and they headed back up the stairs. They stayed focused on the exit route, and nobody stopped them this time. They kept silent until they were inside Sawyer's Maserati.

"That's it?" he confirmed.

"That's it," she told him.

They shared a long look.

"Okay," he said, turning the key. "Okay. Now we find out what we're dealing with here."

Back in Sawyer's penthouse, Niki sat flush against him on the sofa as they shared the diary. It started when Gabriella was twelve, several months after her parents were killed in the interstate pileup and she was left alone. She hadn't written every day, maybe once every couple of weeks.

Obviously, the crash had been terrible. Gabriella had been

lucky, receiving nothing but cuts and bruises. But she'd been placed in a foster home, then another and another. She'd hated them all, the impersonal parents, the hostile children, and the regiment of explaining every detail of her private life to a parade of social workers. The pain and loneliness was clear in her writing.

"Did you know about this?" Sawyer asked in an undertone.

"I knew she was orphaned," Niki answered. "I didn't know she was this unhappy."

They read further, learning how Gabriella had run away from her last foster home. At fifteen, she'd set out to make it on her own. There were a couple of missing months in the diary, but then an entry that talked about a man who was helping her.

He was a banker named Ellis Lorance, and he had an apartment in Georgetown. He also had a wife and family in a suburban neighborhood. Gabriella wrote cheerfully about the gifts he gave her, the fun they had together and his apparent problems with his wife.

"I guess his wife didn't understand him," Niki deadpanned.

"She was so young," said Sawyer.

"Ellis Lorance was a statutory rapist."

"Yes, he was."

"Do you know him?" Niki asked.

Sawyer shook his head.

They read on, coming quickly to the emotional breakup, where a confused Gabriella lost her only support system. Ellis gave her three-hundred dollars and put her out on the street.

Again, there was a missing space of time, until Randal Goddard showed up. This time, Gabriella was more savvy. She asked him to teach her to drive. She opened a bank account and saved part of her spending money. She also chose gifts with lasting value, jewelry instead of clothes, a car instead of a trip, which she made sure was registered in her name.

And that was when she started cataloguing secrets. Randal was the number six partner in a large, Manhattan law firm. He had a wife and two daughters, and Gabriella learned their address and phone number. By the time the relationship ended, Randal was persuaded to give her two months to move out of the apartment and ten-thousand dollars, which Gabriella promptly deposited into her bank account while searching for a new sugar daddy.

"I'm having a hard time blaming her," Sawyer observed.

"She really was thrown to the wolves." Niki liked to think she might have taken the money and gone to a community college in order to get a decent job and become independent. But that didn't seem to be Gabriella's style.

Her next affair was with Neil, a stockbroker with some embarrassing sexual proclivities involving ladies' underwear. At first, Niki squirmed, knowing Sawyer was reading the rather matter-of-fact description about her mother's sex life. But she couldn't help but smile as she read Gabriella's notes about listening and learning about the financial system. Forget college, she realized now how very much her mother had learned about international finance by listening to his phone calls, reading his industry magazines and asking questions.

By the time things ended with Neil, Gabriella had made some very smart investments. She'd also persuaded him to leave her with a sizable check, and her nest egg was well underway.

"Neil Ryland is now the head of Rosewell Demetrick Equities," said Sawyer.

"Do you think he's nervous?"

"I think he's freaking out."

"Yeah, that could be an embarrassing tabloid story."

As the diary went on, Gabriella clearly became more sophisticated and cynical. She never talked about loving or even liking her boyfriends. But she was quite obviously obsessed with financial security. She wrote that if she could get enough money in the bank, she'd never have to depend on anyone ever again.

And then Wilton Terrell came long. Ironically, she seemed to like him. He was gruff and grumpy, but straightforward and honest. He told her she should go back to school and make something of herself. He told her to stop having affairs with married men and get her life under control.

At the same time, going against what seemed to be his own principles, he was sleeping with her. Their affair was short-lived, only a few days, but he had sex with her about a dozen times.

"Hypocritical," Niki observed.

"It seems Gabriella was hard to resist."

"Are you defending your gender?"

"I'm saying we're weak-willed when it comes to beautiful women."

"Girls," Niki corrected. "She was still only eighteen."

"True," Sawyer responded. "You win that one. We're pond scum."

"Thank you for owning up to it."

"Can't say I'm particularly proud of the team at the moment," he mumbled.

When Gabriella found out she was pregnant, she was thrilled. She'd admired Wilton's straightforward honesty, and thought he was good father material.

"Didn't expect that," said Sawyer.

Something warmed inside Niki's chest. "It's nice to know I wasn't unwanted."

"I'm sorry you ever had to feel that way." He stretched his arm across the back of the sofa. "I find I keep contrasting her life to mine when I was a teenager."

"Spoiled little rich boy?"

"You're not far off," he admitted. "Oh, there were pressures, getting into the right schools, the right fraternity, making the rowing team."

"I can only imagine," Niki mocked.

"Hey, you were a spoiled little princess yourself."

"Right. I guess you win that one." Her chest went hollow when she thought of all the sacrifices her mother had made to give her that life.

With Niki on the way, Gabriella became even more obsessed with security. She began picking lovers based on their wealth and their vulnerability. And, after Niki was born, she purposely picked out lovers she could exploit. Using what she'd learned from Neil about investing, and adding to her fortune with ever increasing payoffs from men, Gabriella became a truly wealthy woman.

Niki seemed to be the light of her life, her reason for striving. Not that it was all work, not by any means. Early in the relationships, the men were blissfully ignorant and seemed deliriously happy. They took them on vacations all around the globe, lavished gifts on both Gabriella and Niki.

Eventually, they came to passages where Niki could remember snippets of the story: the first time she was on skis, a sailboat adventure in the Mediterranean, and a trip to Disney World when she was five. It had all looked so innocently different to a small child.

She couldn't help but think about her own life at eleven. How incredibly different it had been from Gabriella's struggle. Her chest went tight, and she had to blink away a rash of tears.

Sawyer slipped the diary out of her hands, setting it down on the coffee table. "We're going to take a break."

But Niki shook her head. She didn't want to stop. Sure, it might be hard, but reading it couldn't possibly be as difficult as living it. She felt honor bound to see this through to the end.

"We're ordering pizza," Sawyer decreed. "And there's some beer in the fridge."

"I'm not hungry," Niki insisted, leaning forward to reach for the diary. This wasn't Sawyer's decision to make.

"You sound like a cranky child."

"I was happy reading."

"You're getting emotionally drained from reading."

"Don't worry about me."

"You need something to eat." He snagged the diary and carried it with him to the telephone near his kitchen.

"You are a bully."

He grinned at her protest. "Maybe so. But I'm acting in your best interest."

"You don't know what I'm feeling."

He sobered, pausing with the telephone receiver in one hand. "Your expression is pretty transparent, Niki. This is hard for you." He glanced at his watch. "And it's nearly seven. And we skipped lunch."

She did feel a pang of hunger, but she swallowed against it.

"Is it so hard to admit I'm right?"

"Yes."

He gave his head a shake of frustration, read a number off a list stuck to his corkboard and dialed the phone.

While they waited for the pizza, Niki retired to the bathroom to freshen up. She changed out of the skirt and sweater in favor of a pair of soft yoga pants and a cropped T-shirt, then splashed water on her face. For the first time since this morning, she let her mind go back to making love with Sawyer.

So much had happened in the past few hours that she hadn't had time to regret it. And, even though she tried now, she couldn't summon up remorse. If anything, she regretted the first time they'd made love, when she found out he was lying to her, and it had spoiled the entire experience.

She gave herself a mental shake. Sawyer was still a liar. He was still the guy who'd hunted her down and spied on her. Maybe he was sexy, and maybe he came across as supportive and kind. But she only had to look as far as her own mother to know that people could act one way and be thinking another.

She shut off the taps and rubbed a towel over her face. She combed her hair and mentally braced herself before returning to Sawyer. He was a good actor, and a great lover, dead stop. Expecting anything else would make her as naive as Gabriella had been when she was fifteen years old.

She found him at the breakfast bar, diary open, making notes.

"I opened one for you." He pointed to a beer bottle.

"What are you doing?" she asked with suspicion.

"Writing down the names of the men so far."

"What are you going to do with that?" Was this the part where his nefarious plan came to light?

"I don't know yet." He put down the pen, closed the diary, then handed Niki a bottle of beer.

It was icy cold in her hand, and she realized she was very thirsty. But she continued to watch him closely.

Sawyer took a drink of his own beer. "I really don't know yet."

"How badly can people hurt me?" she dared ask.

He stilled. "If I have my way, they're not going to hurt you at all."

"But, they'll want to."

"What they want is to save themselves. Randal Goddard is a morally righteous judge and a deacon in his church. His life goes into a tailspin if anyone finds out he slept with a seventeen year old while his wife was pregnant with their third child. Though your mother didn't know it, some of what Neil Ryland did was insider trading. You could spawn an SEC investigation with the blink of an eye."

The doorbell rang, announcing the pizza delivery.

"But, for now," Sawyer finished. "Let's just eat. You're looking a little too thin for my tastes."

"Hey," she protested, reflexively glancing down at herself.

"Don't worry," he called over his shoulder as he crossed to the entry foyer. "I have just the cure."

"Too thin," Niki muttered to herself. "As if." She'd been working on the ranch for months. She had more tone to her muscles than she'd ever had in her life.

Sawyer reappeared with the pizza box.

"Double cheese," he told her, setting it down on the opposite end of the long breakfast bar. "Dense with calories."

Niki took her beer and moved to one of the stools around the counter. Now that she could smell the pizza, she couldn't wait to taste it.

Sawyer set a stoneware plate in front of each of them. "Silverware?" he asked.

"No need." She opened the lid and helped herself to a large gooey slice.

He sat down opposite her. "My kinda girl."

Their gazes met, and they both stilled, as their frantic lovemaking from the morning all but sizzled between them.

"I have no idea what to do with you," he told her with a dark intensity.

She struggled to shake off her feelings. She was falling too fast and too hard for Sawyer Layton. She knew he'd lied to her, had been operating against her. But she believed him when he said he hadn't expected the attraction between them. His actions rang true in that. He had tried to stop their lovemaking. He had backed off on their first kiss.

And now he seemed to be helping her. He claimed he wasn't trying to hurt her, and she was starting to believe him. She was starting to believe him, even though she knew that line of thinking wasn't healthy. It wasn't even safe.

From somewhere deep inside, maybe from that self-preservation taught to her by Gabriella, she found a flippant voice. "I'm not yours to do anything with," she told him.

Then she bit down on her pizza, looking away.

"Not yet," she thought she heard him mumble.

But when she glanced at him, he was focused on handling a slice of pizza.

"What?" he asked, looking up. "You expecting an argument?"

"Delicious," she said instead of responding.

"Aldo's," he told her. "My favorite."

"Can't get pizza like this in Lyndon Valley." She took another big bite.

After the pizza, they went back to the diary. As Niki grew older, things got tougher for Gabriella. Eventually, she chose the wrong man. He abused her, and when she tried to get away, he revealed his connections to corrupt police officers.

"That was the year we went to Rio," Niki whispered in horror. "She pulled me out of third grade in October, and we took off for months."

Eventually, Gabriella had found herself a bigger, badder lover, and the man who'd beat her backed off. She struggled with the fine lines between sex, coercion and an almost maniacal desire to party and to protect Niki.

"She adored you," Sawyer observed.

"How did she do it?" Niki wondered out loud. "Some of these guys were really scary."

"Ironic that what she was seeking was safety."

It became clear as the diary went on, that no amount of money was ever going to be enough for Gabriella. She worried that she and Niki would have to disappear, and she worried that powerful people would be searching for them, making it even harder to hide.

"She seemed so carefree." Niki found herself reframing much of her childhood, seeing her mother through a different lens. Her heart ached as she thought of her mother never having anyone to confide in, not even her own daughter.

When Sawyer suggested they go to bed and finish reading in the morning, Niki agreed. And when he took her hand and led her to his own room, she didn't protest.

They took off their clothes and climbed under the quilt, and he drew her back against his body, spooning her, kissing her, wishing her a good night.

Sawyer lay still in his bed with Niki cradled in his arms. She'd fallen asleep almost instantly. He'd dozed off and on, but mostly he'd lain awake trying to come up with his next move.

Over the course of the afternoon and evening, he'd developed a grim admiration for Gabriella. He felt strangely protective of the young woman he'd come to know through the pages of her diary. One thing was for sure. Nobody but Niki had the right to read what she'd written.

He felt his arms tighten around Niki. He knew he'd protect her to his dying breath. Maybe if someone had loved Gabriella the way he loved Niki, her life would have turned out differently.

Sawyer held on to that thought for a long moment. He loved Niki. When he suggested they disappear together, he'd been completely serious. He'd run off with her in a heartbeat, leave his entire life behind and never look back.

While he knew he could do it, he doubted Niki would be willing to leave her newly found family in Colorado. So, for now, he was calling that Plan B.

She moved against him in her sleep and, for about the hundredth time, he wished he could shift her onto her back and make slow, sweet love to her. But that wasn't what she needed. She didn't need a man who would take from her and not give back. She needed someone who would put her first. And Sawyer would do that for her. The next few days were going to be all about Niki.

He glanced at the glowing clock beside his bed. It was coming up on seven. Another day was about to start, and he needed to use it wisely.

She stirred again, shifting onto her back, and her eyes fluttered open to focus on him. All he could think was how much he loved her and how ridiculously happy it made him to have her here.

"We slept," she whispered.

"We did," he agreed.

"I thought…"

He smiled at her hesitation. "You thought I'd ravish you?"

"You do seem to like ravishing."

He knew now wasn't the time for lovemaking. He needed to think, and she needed to get her emotions back in order. And they both needed to finish reading before they could move on to anything.

"Shower's through there." He pointed to the door to the en suite.

She glanced to the hallway. "I can use—"

"No," he interrupted. "Stay here. Use my shower."

There was still a trace of confusion in her eyes. He couldn't blame her. She probably wasn't sure if they were adversaries, allies or lovers. He'd been confused, too. But now he knew they were all of those things, and so much more.

She slipped out of his bed, and he enjoyed the view as she walked naked to the en suite. Then he ruthlessly turned his mind to Gabriella's former lovers.

He knew they would all want to save themselves. While some of them, his uncle, for example, would want to hurt each other. They could destroy one another for all Sawyer cared, so long as Niki didn't get caught in the crossfire.

Then Sawyer stilled. His brow popped up. Yes, some would want to hurt each other.

He'd been coming at this all wrong. He didn't need to convince these men that Niki was harmless. He needed to replace her with their real enemy.

Twelve

Niki was more than relieved when the diary's story got better. Though there were several more men, Sawyer's uncle included, eventually Gabriella recognized that she didn't need the men in order to multiply her fortune. She continued to be a shrewd investor, and the money in Switzerland turned into more than she and Niki would ever need or want.

This was the part Niki remembered most clearly, her and Gabriella on their own, partying their way around the world. Niki cramming for exams while they rushed back to Melbourne Academy so that she could write them and pass onto the next year.

"She was hardly a textbook mother, was she?" Sawyer asked while they sat once again on the couch, sharing the pages.

"It was out of control at times, but a whole lot of fun. Sometimes, I used to wish she was someone else. But, she wasn't. She was her own crazy, mixed-up person who wanted to drag every second of joy out of her life."

"I'd say she did it," said Sawyer. "You were the best thing that ever happened to her."

"We were best friends for a lot of years."

"You must miss her." Sawyer's tone was sympathetic as he turned the final page.

"I do," Niki agreed. Some days, she ached with missing her.

"She would want you to be happy now."

Niki tipped her head up to look at him. "She would want me to be strong."

"You are strong." He paused for a moment. "And I'm going to need your help."

Niki listened in growing astonishment as Sawyer outlined his plan.

When Sawyer and Niki entered the private meeting room, the fourteen men around the boardroom table gaped at her in obvious astonishment. Sawyer knew they had to have their suspicions about why he'd called them here. But they sure hadn't expected he'd produce Niki herself.

"Gentlemen," Sawyer opened, motioning for Niki to take one of the two chairs at the head of the table. "I'm sure you all recognize Niki Gerard."

"Well done, nephew," Charles boomed from the chair at the opposite end of the table.

Sawyer glared at his uncle, taking his own seat next to Niki and pointedly placing the diary down in front of her.

All eyes moved to stare at it.

"Yes," he answered their unspoken question. "It is."

"And it's ours," announced Charles, emphasizing each word. "My nephew delivered, just like I knew he would." His uncle's gaze came to rest disdainfully on Niki.

"Stop talking. Now," Sawyer ordered. "Niki has something to say."

He shifted to take in her expression, hoping she wasn't intimidated by the group of obviously anxious men.

She wasn't. Her face was calm as she looked from Judge

Goddard and Judge Needly, to Neil Ryland, Ellis Lorance, Congressman Harbottle, Carter, Furlo, Koeper, Newlin and all the others.

"I read the diary," she told them all. "I know who you are and what you did."

"Wait just a—"

"Be quiet," Sawyer interrupted Judge Goddard.

"You used a young woman," Niki continued. Her tone was low, and they had to strain to hear. "And in some cases, a young girl. You cheated on your families. You lied to your companies, to your voters, to the public." Niki tapped her finger on the diary and gave a light laugh. "My first instinct was to make you feel guilty. But then it occurred to me that you are incapable of guilt. The only emotion you understand is fear."

A few people shifted in their chairs.

In his peripheral vision, Sawyer saw the smug smile that grew on Uncle Charles's face. "Don't mess with the Laytons," he intoned.

"That's enough," Sawyer ground out.

"People need to know we're capable," Charles persisted. "That you and I worked together, tracked her down, executed a textbook plan."

"We found Niki," Sawyer allowed, hoping that would be enough for Charles.

But Charles let his gaze circle the room. "The Laytons have the information now—"

"Is this a shakedown?" Ellis Lorance demanded.

"I don't want your money," said Niki.

"I want your endorsement," said Charles. "In the campaign."

"Nobody's shaking anybody down for anything," Sawyer told them with conviction.

Charles smirked. "Say whatever it is you need to say, Sawyer."

But it was Niki who spoke next. "None of you will *ever* gain advantage from this book. Sawyer and I agreed. We agreed."

"We?" Charles piped in. "There is no *we,* honey. My nephew

found you. He romanced you. He exploited you. And he got exactly what the family needed."

With surprising speed, Charles stood and rounded the table, snagged the diary. "You should all be very afraid," he told the assembled group. "The Laytons are in charge now."

"Sawyer?" Niki's voice beside him was small.

He glanced down and saw the uncertainty in her eyes. "Charles is wrong," he assured her. "He's lying right now to—"

"He said he'd date you if he had to," Charles interrupted. "But only if he had to. How do you think it happened, sweetheart? He turned on a dime there, didn't he, turning you into a couple? Why do you think his first stop in D.C. was my house?"

Sawyer was hard-pressed not to throttle his uncle. But Niki was on her feet, heading for the door.

Sawyer wrestled the diary from his uncle's grip. His first instinct was to go after her. But he wasn't finished there just yet.

The evening sun was warm. The air was clear. The flowers were in full bloom, and the honeybees were buzzing from blossom to blossom. It was a beautiful, bucolic scene, but none of it could chase away Niki's sadness.

"We could go riding again," said Travis, coming up beside her on the little bridge over the creek next to Reed's half-built house.

"You don't need to babysit me," she told him. "I know I'm a downer."

The last of the work crew was packing up for the day. Truck doors were slamming, and engines were starting.

"We lonely singles have to stick together. I love my sisters. But they're pretty happy and insufferable at the moment."

Niki tried to muster a smile at his joke, but it turned watery. She had to admit, watching Reed and Katrina together right now, or Mandy and Caleb for that matter, wasn't the easiest thing in the world. Their intimate smiles, little touches, quick kisses and shared whispers reminded Niki of Sawyer and what she'd never have again.

It had been nearly a week since she'd walked out of the meeting, but her pain felt as raw as that first day. She'd called her brothers, and Caleb had flown her home.

And it was home. A home like she'd never known before. She couldn't help but think that her mother would be happy that she was out from under the men of D.C., and had found such a wonderful family.

But at night, close to sleep, she couldn't help traveling back to D.C., imagining Sawyer's arms around her, his gravelly voice in her ear, his fingertips touching, lips kissing, and then she'd startle awake and discover she was all alone.

"Hey." Travis put a companionable arm around her shoulders. "You're going to survive this. I promise you will. Nobody ever really died of a broken heart."

"It's not broken," Niki insisted, more to herself than to him. She was tough, tougher than she had ever imagined. She was not going to be one of those women who mooned over the loss of a man.

"Bruised, then."

"Callused."

There was a smile in his voice. "Tough as a cowboy's rearend?"

"Shoe leather," she insisted.

"Sure it is," he agreed.

"Don't humor me."

"What do you want me to do?" He pulled back to look at her, hands on her shoulders. "Come on, Niki. Tell me how to help."

Before she could answer, she caught a glimpse of movement behind his shoulder. She squinted. The distant man's stride was familiar, and her stomach all but sank to her toes.

She blinked desperately against the setting sun, certain her eyes were playing tricks. But, no. He was still there, still walking toward them, long strides eating up the meadow between.

"Kiss me," she told Travis.

"What?"

"Right now. Kiss me like you mean it."

"That's not a very good—"

"Do it."

Sawyer was closing in.

"Niki, something on the rebound is not—"

"He's *here,*" she hissed.

"Who's where?"

"Sawyer."

Travis's head twitched.

"Don't look."

"I won't."

"Please, Travis. Don't let me look pathetic." She couldn't let Sawyer guess how badly she'd fallen for his romantic deception.

A smile grew on Travis's face. "You could never look pathetic. But if it's what you want."

Without another word, he wrapped his arms around her and tipped his head toward her, touching his lips to hers. The kiss itself was quite chaste, but his hug was enveloping, and he bent her slightly backward over his forearm.

Niki closed her eyes, Travis's kiss slipping into the background, every other sense attuned to Sawyer's approach.

His foot clunked on the footbridge, and she swore she could catch his scent on the wind.

Travis slowly broke the kiss. Then he winked at Niki before turning to meet Sawyer, one arm looped loosely around her waist.

Niki blinked the world back into focus, her gaze catching and holding on Sawyer's grim glare.

"Hey, Sawyer," Travis drawled.

She couldn't force herself to speak.

Travis casually tucked her hair behind one ear, leaning in to whisper, "I think he wants to take me apart."

Her heart clenched.

"Hello, Niki." Sawyer's tone seemed almost dire.

"Hello," she managed, despite paper-dry vocal cords.

"I had hoped you'd wait," he said.

"Wait for what?"

"For me to explain what my uncle said."

"She got tired of waiting," Travis put in.

Niki couldn't imagine what Sawyer could possibly explain. He'd plotted against her all along, kept his uncle in the loop, told him the romance was a farce.

"You've got a lot of nerve showing up here," said Travis.

Sawyer's attention swung to Travis, his hands going to his hips. "You've got a lot of nerve, period."

"She's made her choice," said Travis, his arm tightening possessively on Niki.

"Is that the truth?" Sawyer asked her.

Though everything inside Niki urged her to push away from Travis and throw herself into Sawyer's arms, she stood her ground. There was nothing left to salvage in this but her pride.

"Travis doesn't lie to me," she said.

Sawyer's hard gaze narrowed. "So, that's it? We're done?"

"Done?" Her tone was incredulous. "Sawyer, we never even started." She couldn't figure out what he was doing here. He'd gotten what he wanted. What was the point of dragging it out?

"There's more than one version of what happened between us." He paused on purpose, but she didn't know what he was expecting her to say.

"So, that's a yes," he finished.

Niki looked away. "That's a yes," she told Sawyer, feeling as though something inside her had died.

He stared at her for a long moment. A horse whinnied softly in the distance, and the breeze swirled the scent of sweet clover.

His hands dropped to his sides. "Well, then there's one final thing you should know," he said. "They won't bother you again."

"You mean *you* won't bother me again."

Sawyer looked momentarily confused. "Yeah, well, that, too. But I mean the men in the diary. They're all backing off."

His gaze took in Travis, then moved back to her. "They'll never, ever bother you from now on."

"Even your uncle?"

"Especially my uncle."

Curiosity got the better of her. "What did you do?"

"What we said we'd do."

Travis was obviously curious as well because he asked, "Which was what?"

"Destroy the diary," she and Sawyer answered together.

"It's gone for good," said Sawyer. "Nobody but Niki and I will ever read it."

Niki knew it was for the best, but she couldn't quash the crushing sense of disappointment. She'd never read her mother's words again.

"She's free." Sawyer's jaw clamped down. His nostrils flared and a muscle twitched next to his eye. "And I guess she's yours."

He gazed at Niki for the last time, seeming to drink in every inch of her. Then he turned to walk off the bridge.

Silence was left in his wake.

Travis broke it. "Are you just going to stand there?"

"I should thank him," she breathed.

"I don't think he wants a thank-you."

Travis gazed meaningfully down at her. "He could have sent you an email to tell you about the diary. He came all the way out here. He wanted to see you."

"I don't understand," said Niki, her mind searching for sense in Sawyer's words. "Did I hear that right?"

"He didn't betray you."

She shook her head in denial. "That doesn't follow." All along, Sawyer had been operating in his own interest, not in hers.

"Yes, it does," said Travis. "At least, it does if he's in love with you."

"No." It couldn't be. It couldn't possibly be.

"He just chose you over his own uncle."

"It has to be a trick."

"He's getting away," Travis pointed out.

She swore under her breath. She didn't know what to think. She didn't know what to do.

"What if you're wrong?" she whispered to Travis.

"What if I'm right?"

Suddenly, Niki took a step forward, then another and another. Then she was running, trying to catch Sawyer who was halfway up the rise, halfway to his pickup truck where he'd drive out of her life forever.

The ground was uneven, and her legs felt like lead. She twisted an ankle, but quickly righted herself, cursing the fact that it was uphill and that her legs were so much shorter than his.

She finally caught him at the edge of the driveway, snagging his arm.

He swung around, and they both stared at each other.

Her heart was thudding, her palms sweating. She was battling hope, while desperately trying to brace herself. She was brave, but not when it came to Sawyer. She loved him so much, and she was so frightened of being hurt.

"Why did you come?" she managed to ask.

"I hoped you'd forgive me." His gaze moved over her shoulder to Travis. "But it looks like I'm too late."

"Forgive you for what? For lying to me? For manipulating me? For sleeping with me?"

He reached for her arm, and sensation flowed over her skin, through to her heart. The wind whispered between them.

"For falling in love with you," he finally said. "For figuring out what was happening between us. For trying to give us a chance to be together."

It was true? He loved her? He *loved* her? She tried to speak, but nothing came out.

"I've wasted my time."

"I love you, Sawyer," she admitted in a rush. "Forever and always."

"Then why were you kissing Travis?"

Her eyes widened. "We were faking it."

"That wasn't fake."

"The kiss was real," she admitted. "But we're only friends, closer to siblings than anything. He was helping me salvage my pride."

"Very gentlemanly of him," Sawyer ground out.

"It was."

"Don't do it again."

"I won't."

"I love you, Niki."

A smile stretched across her face. "I can't even believe it."

"How can I prove it?"

"Since we can do anything and go anywhere, and we don't have to hide anymore, you can take me golfing."

Sawyer coughed out a surprised laugh.

"Take me to Wailea," she clarified.

"Nothing in the world I'd rather do." He moved in and kissed her again. This time he kissed her long and hard and deeply.

Minutes rolled by as they clung together, and satisfying passion took over her system.

Footfalls sounded on the ground, growing closer. "Get a room," Travis's voice interrupted.

"I think we'll need a suite," Sawyer responded, drawing back to gaze lovingly into Niki's eyes, smoothing back her hair, cupping her face.

Then he looked at Travis. "You know, you're lucky to be alive."

Travis was completely unrepentant. "Figured it was worth the risk."

"You think of her as a sister?"

"Always will."

"Okay," Sawyer nodded.

Travis grinned. "She's all yours."

"Hey!" Niki protested their cavalier attitude.

"What?" Sawyer glanced down. "You think there's any chance in the world I'm giving you up?"

Epilogue

Their penthouse suite at the Wailea Sapphire Hotel overlooked the beach on one side and the fairway of the sixth hole on the other. The three rooms were spacious, classy and comfortable. But the real feature was the veranda. Long and wide, it wrapped around the corner of the building. It featured lounge chairs, a dining table, a hot tub and views extending miles out into the Pacific.

They'd only arrived on Maui this morning, but they'd already played nine holes of golf, skipped along the shoreline in a compact catamaran, gone snorkeling on the reef and swam in the warm waves at dusk. Afterward, at Sawyer's insistence, Niki had changed into a flowing white cotton dress they'd purchased at a high-end hotel shop. Sawyer had gone with khakis and a short-sleeved shirt.

Their early dinner had been served on the private deck by an efficient butler and two assistants. Now, with the servers and dishes cleared away, they stood side by side at the rail gazing over the beachfront, while the sun slid down to the watery horizon.

Niki wasn't sure she'd ever been this content.

"Is that what I think it is?" she whispered to Sawyer, leaning up against his arm.

"Somebody's getting married."

While they watched, a group of hotel attendants wove flowers into a white, latticework archway. Others were setting up chairs, and a pathway of torches leading from the hotel.

"That's the way to do it." Niki sighed. "No muss, no fuss. Just a few good friends on a beach."

"You'd like that?" he asked her in a low tone.

"I would."

He turned to face her. "I have a present for you."

"You don't think flying to Maui, a luxurious penthouse, golfing, and a candle-lit five-course dinner is enough for one day?"

"No, I don't believe it is."

"Well, I can't think of a single thing that's missing."

Sawyer gave a slow smile, reaching over to the table, extracting a wrapped package from beneath a napkin. It was compact and flat, about eight inches long. The embossed, silver wrapping paper glinted in the candlelight.

"You didn't need to do this." Niki tugged on the delicate bow.

"I don't need to do anything," he told her. "Not anymore. Now it's all about what I want to do."

"That seems rather self-indulgent."

"There's nothing wrong with a little self-indulgence."

She peeled back the edges of the paper, eager to discover what he'd chosen. The paper fell away to reveal a plain white box.

Puzzled, she lifted the lid.

She had to blink. Then she moved closer to the candles on the table, angling the box. "Is it?"

"Yes, it is."

Niki reached out to run her fingertip across the tan leather of Gabriella's diary. "I thought you said you destroyed it like we planned."

"It's yours, Niki. Nobody but you has any right to do anything with it."

An unexpected surge of emotion overtook her. She reflexively pulled the diary against her chest and held it there, feeling close to her mother once again.

"You okay?" Sawyer moved to draw her into his embrace.

"Fine," she whispered, tears clogging her throat.

"I didn't mean to upset you."

She shook her head in denial, leaning into him. "You didn't. It's good. Thank you," she whispered.

"You're happy?"

"So happy."

He gently extracted the box from her hand, setting everything down on the table, so they could hug each other properly. "Making you happy is all I want to do."

"You've succeeded."

He took her left hand, brought it to his lips, and before she knew what was happening, he'd slipped something cool onto her finger.

"What?" She pulled free, only to find a large diamond winking at her from her ring finger.

She stared at him in disbelief, and he grinned unrepentantly back.

"Isn't there supposed to be a question that comes along with this?" she asked, her brain struggling to accept what the ring had to mean.

"You think I'd give you a chance to say no?"

"You want to marry me?" She didn't know if she needed to confirm it in words.

"I want to marry you," he echoed. "No, wait. I'm *going* to marry you."

He turned her back to the beach where the wedding preparations were still underway.

"I hope you don't mind," said Sawyer. "But that down there, it's for us."

"The wedding?" She gave her head a small shake.

"The wedding," he confirmed.

"Oh, you're joking." She tried to laugh.

"I'm not joking, Niki. Caleb flew your family in this afternoon."

Her gaze went back to the picture-perfect wedding on the beach. "You're serious?"

"I'm serious."

"What if I'd said no?"

"You weren't going to say no."

"You're right," she agreed. "I would never say no." The contentment in her chest turned to full out joy. "I love you, Sawyer Layton."

His arm went around her. "I love you, Niki Gerard." He nodded to the beach. "Look. There they are."

The staff lit the torches, and a group of people made their way to the folding chairs. She easily picked out Reed, Caleb and Travis.

"I better get down there," said Sawyer. "Dylan's meeting me with the rings."

There was a knock on the door.

"That'll be Katrina," he told Niki. "She's got your flowers."

Niki felt like the world was spinning around her. "We're really doing this? We're getting married right now?"

"Right now," Sawyer confirmed with an unabashed grin. "Then we're going back to Lyndon Valley. I'm keeping the ranch. The rest we can make up as we go along."

"I love being near my brothers," Niki admitted on a sigh.

"And I love being near you."

The knock sounded again.

Sawyer reached for her hands. "You look beautiful, sweetheart."

"This is why you insisted on this particular dress."

"This is why I insisted on you."

She wrapped her arms around his neck and squeezed hard. "I love you, Sawyer."

He held her tight. "Then let's make it official and forever."

* * * * *